"What Do You Want Me To Say, Jess?"

Devlin asked with quiet savagery. "That I hate waking up every morning of my life because it means facing another day without you? That there hasn't been a night in eight years that I haven't dreamed of you? A woman I didn't pretend was you?" His fingers gripped her arms.

His breath curled around the side of her throat, warm and moist, and she froze as he whispered ferociously, "Do you want me to tell you that just seeing you here brings it all back? That I'd like to lay you down on this rug and—"

"Mommy!" The voice came floating through the screen door, and Jess felt Devlin stiffen. Footsteps pounded across the veranda and an instant later the door banged open and Heather came flying into the room. "Mommy, someone's coming!" Heather saw Dev then and careened to a stop, her eyes widening. . . .

Dear Reader:

Sensuous, emotional, compelling... these are all words that describe Silhouette Desire. If this is your first Desire novel, let me extend an invitation for you to sit back, kick off your shoes and revel in the pleasure of a tantalizing, fulfilling love story. If you're a regular reader, you already know that you're in for a real treat!

A Silhouette Desire can encompass many varying moods and tones. The story can be deeply moving and dramatic, or charming and lighthearted. But no matter what, each and every Silhouette Desire is a terrific romance written by and for today's woman.

I know you'll love March's *Man of the Month* book, *McAllister's Lady* by Naomi Horton. Also, look for *Granite Man*, one of Elizabeth Lowell's WESTERN LOVERS series. And don't miss wonderful love stories by some undeniable favorites *and* exciting newcomers: Kelly Jamison, Lucy Gordon, Beverly Barton and Karen Leabo.

So give in to Desire... you'll be glad you did!

All the best,

Lucia Macro
Senior Editor

NAOMI HORTON

McALLISTER'S LADY

SILHOUETTE *Desire*®

Published by Silhouette Books New York

America's Publisher of Contemporary Romance

SILHOUETTE BOOKS
300 East 42nd St., New York, N.Y. 10017

McALLISTER'S LADY

ISBN: 0-373-05630-3

First Silhouette Books printing March 1991

Books by Naomi Horton

Silhouette Romance

Risk Factor #342

Silhouette Desire

Dream Builder #161
River of Dreams #236
Split Images #269
Star Light, Star Bright #302
Lady Liberty #320
No Walls Between Us #365
Pure Chemistry #386
Crossfire #435
A Dangerous Kind of Man #487
The Ideal Man #518
Cat's Play #596
McAllister's Lady #630

Silhouette Intimate Moments

Strangers No More #323
In Safekeeping #343

NAOMI HORTON

was born in northern Alberta, where the winters are long and the libraries far apart. "When I'd run out of books," she says, "I'd simply create my own—entire worlds filled with people, adventure and romance. I guess it's not surprising that I'm still at it!" An engineering technologist, she presently lives in Nanaimo, British Columbia, with her collection of assorted pets.

For my editor, Paula,
a kindred spirit and fellow romantic
who makes writing even the most difficult books
a little easier—for trusting me,
and for trusting the man who stole
both our hearts, Dev McAllister.

Prologue

"**I**'m scared." The little girl's voice wavered. Her eyes were the color of forget-me-nots, wide and very frightened. "If he finds us, he's going to hurt Mommy and me."

"He's not going to hurt you, Shelley." Dev said the words with flat conviction, not as comfort but as hard, cold fact. He knelt in front of Shelley, looking down into those frightened blue eyes. "I gave you my word when I brought you and your mother here. He won't find you—that's why this place is called a safe house. We're going to stay here until they find him and put him in jail. Then it'll be over...."

"We'll be all right, Lieutenant McAllister." Shelley's mother managed a wan smile.

Dev smiled across the child's head. Laurel Conroy was as dark-haired as her daughter was fair, with a shy half smile and eyes as wide and frightened as Shelley's. "It's Dev, remember?"

She smiled that sweet, hesitant smile, and Dev felt his stomach constrict. Jess, he found himself thinking inanely for the hundredth time since he'd met her. *She looks just like Jess....*

He shook it off irritably, annoyed at his own rambling thoughts. He was a cop, and a damned good one. Too good to let a few stray memories mess up his concentration. He was here to protect Laurel Conroy from the estranged husband who had threatened to kill both her and the child, and the fact that she had the same silken dark hair and shy smile and small, oval face as a woman he hadn't seen in nearly seven years didn't figure into it.

"You're going to stay here, aren't you?" Shelley gazed at him anxiously, hugging her doll, Miss Patticakes, tightly against her.

"You bet I am," Dev told her with a reassuring smile.

Shelley nodded doubtfully, hugging Miss Patticakes a little tighter, and Dev sighed. How do you tell a five-year-old kid whose own father was threatening to kill her that everything's going to be all right? That kind of betrayal cuts deep, shaking the very foundations of a child's world, and it wasn't something a few words from a well-meaning stranger could mend.

"I'll tell you what," he said suddenly. "I'm going to give you a magic talisman. How does that sound?" He drew the cuff of his jacket back to expose the narrow gold link ID bracelet on his left wrist. It was the one that Jess had given him over ten years ago; the one he'd never quite been able to throw out with the rest of the memories. He didn't even know why he still wore the damned thing. Except maybe just to taunt himself....

He shook the memories off impatiently and undid the clasp. "It's got my name written on it, see?" He held it up so Shelley could see the script, then motioned for her to hold out her arm. "Now this is a very special bracelet," he told her seriously. Gently, he wrapped the chain around her tiny wrist until it was snug, then fastened it. "It's got some heavy-duty magic on it, and I can promise you that as long as you're wearing it, nothing is going to hurt you."

"Really?" Her eyes widened and she touched the bracelet almost reverently. "Thank you," she replied solemnly,
holding up her arm so the sunlight glinted off gold. "See,
Mommy?"

"I see it, darling." Dev could see the glimmer of unshed
tears in Laurel's eyes as she looked across her daughter's
head at him. "Thank you," she whispered. "I don't know
how to thank you for everything. For making us feel
safe...."

Dev smiled and eased himself to his feet, looking at the
little girl standing in front of him. She was gazing at him
with an expression of such uncomplicated trust on her up-
turned face that Dev felt his heart give a twist. Trust that
deep, that certain, had to be treated like the precious gift it
was, and he smiled as he reached out and brushed a forgotten tear from her cheek. "You don't worry about a thing,
okay? Not while I'm here. Because Dev McAllister isn't
going to let anything happen to you, and that's a promise...."

"No...oh, God, no...."

It was his own voice, thick with horror. But Dev hardly
heard it. He was staring at the glittering thing that had fallen
out of the envelope when he'd opened it.

It was the bracelet. That damned ID bracelet....

He stared at it where it had fallen, lying between his feet
like a puddle of gold against the faded colors of the rag rug.

The letter lay beside it. It had drifted out of his numbed
fingers and he'd sat there and watched it fall, feeling sick
and cold. They'd found it, the letter said, when they'd finally gone through their daughter's things. And those of her
daughter, their only grandchild.

It had taken them a year of grieving before they'd been
able to bring themselves to do it, and they'd found the
bracelet among the few personal things the police had given
them after...well, afterward. They'd recognized the name
and had thought he might want it back. And they were

praying for him, they added. Praying that he might find the peace they finally had. That he might forgive them for the things they'd said and, finally, that he might forgive himself....

Dev swallowed at the rising sickness, fighting it and the memories that closed around him, plucking at the edges of his mind with their cold, bloodless fingers. Memories of that day a year ago when promises had turned to lies, and a small child's laughter had been stilled forever.

He gave a low groan, trying not to think of two wide blue eyes looking trustingly up into his. His hands tightened on the glass and he lifted it, took a deep swallow of the bourbon. It burned his throat and he coughed raggedly, fighting to keep it down.

It wouldn't work, of course. There wasn't enough bourbon in the world to keep the memories at bay forever. The best he could hope for was a day or two of oblivion, and a handful of dreamless nights.

Smiling grimly, he reached across for the bottle. For now, that was enough. For now, that's all he needed....

One

He was drunk when she found him. Drunker than anyone she'd ever seen.

His pickup truck was there, its grille bent around the gate-post, driver's door gaping. It was out of gas and the head-lights were so dim she realized it had been sitting there, abandoned and running, for hours. She reached inside and turned the ignition and lights off, then closed the door and went to look for him.

He wasn't hard to find, even in the dark and pelting rain. He was lying in the ditch just on the other side of the gate, sprawled out in the mud on his belly, one hand still clutched around the neck of a broken whiskey bottle.

There was a swelling bruise on his forehead, but aside from that he didn't seem to be hurt. His breathing was deep and regular, and when she placed her fingertips against the pulse in his throat, his heartbeat was strong. It was only then that she realized his left hand was bleeding where it was still gripping the neck of the broken bottle.

Carefully, she eased it out of his hand and examined the gash on his palm. It was a clean cut, not too deep, and she decided to leave it until she got him up to the house, letting the rain wash it clean. His face was heavily stubbled with two or three days' worth of beard and from the state of his clothing, she doubted he'd slept or changed in that time, either.

"Oh, Dev," she whispered, her eyes prickling with tears as she gazed down at him. "What have you done to yourself, Dev? You're supposed to be the strong one, remember? You were the one who was always going to be there for me if I needed you."

She smoothed a handful of thick, rain-wet hair from his forehead, the touch turning into a caress. Even now, she had to touch him. He murmured something thickly and tried to turn his head away, and she sighed and got to her feet, stumbling a little in the slick mud.

It was still raining and she combed her own soaking hair back from her face with her fingers, staring down at the man lying in the mud at her feet. The man she'd once loved more than anyone in the world; the man whose child she'd borne.

They were linked, Devlin and her. In ways she wasn't even certain she understood. She, and Dev, and Gary. The three of them had once been inseparable: she'd loved them both and had been forced to choose; had married one but had lain awake nights dreaming of the other.

The three of them had drifted within each other's orbits like captured comets, twisting love into hate, and hate into vengeance, and vengeance into . . . what?

It was desperation that had brought her out here from Seattle to Whiskey Island to find a man she knew hated her with as much passion as he'd once loved. He'd moved out to the San Juan Islands to escape a nightmare, retreating not just from his past but from everyone and everything associated with it, hurting with the kind of emotional pain that a man should never have to endure.

But even knowing that hadn't stopped her. There were only she and Dev now. Drawn together even now by the third.

Gary's death had freed her even as it had imprisoned Dev. She still had a daughter to live for. But Dev? What did he have now? Not even the hate that had given as much meaning to his life as love had once done.

Is that what he'd been searching for in the depths of that whiskey bottle, she found herself wondering. Answers to questions no man should have to ask? Absolution? Or simple oblivion? And if she brought him back and asked him to help her, what was it going to cost both of them?

He dreamed there was a woman there.

As soft as a woman should be, and sweet smelling. She whispered things to him, coaxing things, and in his dream the two of them were struggling through mud and pelting rain toward a distant light that turned out to be nothing more than his own house, the door wide-open as he'd left it, the bare porch bulb a beacon through nightmare.

He reached for her and she came to him, as a woman should in a dream. Her skin was like silk, and her breasts, when he groped through the darkness for them, full and heavy and tasting of honey. And she was easing him out of his clothes until he was naked, wanting her, reaching for her, his body responding strongly in spite of the liquor, but when he tried to draw her over him she slipped through his fingers like mist and he swore at her, called her things he'd called another woman once. Things no man should utter, no woman should hear.

And then he was in the shower, although he had no recollection of how he'd gotten there. The water was copious and hot and he stood there for a long, long while, arms braced against the cool tile wall as the woman, his dream woman, rubbed silken hands over him, soaping him down, rinsing him as the water pounded down over the two of them. He watched it swirl around his feet, discolored by blood, and wondered, absently, if it was his and, if so, why he felt nothing.

The hands moved over him with disturbing familiarity, impersonal and yet gentle, too, and when he turned clumsily he found her there with him, naked but for a light cotton bra and panties, and when he reached for her this time he found not mist but lush, warm flesh. And then she, too, was suddenly naked and he was making love to her, clumsily and not particularly well, too drunk for finesse, too fargone to manage more than a token attempt to satisfy even himself.

He gave up finally and turned away from her, blinded by the hot water, wanting nothing more than the sweet oblivion of sleep or unconsciousness or even death. Anything to blot out the sound of soft weeping that could have been hers or could, even, have been his own.

But then the small, strong hands were tugging at him again and she was urging him out of the tub, swearing at him, her voice cutting through the sleepy fog. He managed to stay on his feet somehow, fumbling ineffectually with the heavy towel she handed him until in frustration she dried him off herself, swearing at him and slapping his hands away as he reached for the softness of her breasts.

And then, finally, she let him go and he went tumbling, tumbling down into the shadowed, quiet darkness he'd been seeking all along. There was nothing down there: no dreams, no memories, nothing at all waiting to ambush him. He remembered those oddly familiar hands tugging a sheet and blanket around him, easing a pillow under his head. And he thought, as he slipped at last down into that dark, silent place, that he felt the feather touch of lips against his cheek and he whispered a name—a name he'd not spoken in eight years—and then he simply let the swirling darkness wash over him until nothing at all remained.

It was the sunlight that wakened him.

Sharp, brittle shards of sunlight that pierced his eyelids like broken glass. He groaned and turned his head, trying to get away from it.

Big mistake. The pain lanced through him, bright as fire, and he groaned again. He lay there, as still as death, until the worst of it eased.

Dev opened one eye finally, cautiously, not entirely convinced he could manage even that much without doing himself serious harm.

The room was his, all right. Living room. Tidier maybe than the last time he'd seen it, but hell, that had been, what . . . a couple of days and a few bottles of bourbon ago, so anything could have happened.

It took a long while for him to gather the courage to open the other eye. Immediately regretting it, he gave a grunt of pain and covered his eyes with his arm to shut out the sunlight.

So. He'd come through it more or less in one piece. That meant the agony in his head, throughout his entire body, wouldn't last forever.

Slowly, teeth gritted, he eased his legs over the edge of the sofa and sat up. Wished he hadn't as the entire room started to swing perilously and his stomach gave a rebellious heave.

"Oh, God. . . ."

It may have been his voice. The sound reverberated inside his skull and he let his head sag forward, cradling it between his hands, elbows braced none-too-steadily on his knees. He managed to open his eyes after a long while and stared at the faded braid rug between his feet.

Another pair of feet appeared suddenly in front of him. Small feet tidily enclosed in pink sneakers. Women's sneakers. Lord, who? He racked his throbbing mind for a name, a face, a memory—anything. Had he met her at a bar and brought her home? He vaguely remembered a dismal—and unsuccessful—attempt at lovemaking last night—had it been last night?—but beyond that was just a merciful blank.

"Here. Try this. It might help." A mug appeared in front of him, containing something milky that fizzled unpleasantly.

"Cyanide?" he croaked hopefully.

There was a snort of not-entirely sympathetic female laughter. "Drink it."

It was less effort to do as she said than to argue and he reached for the mug, took a deep breath to brace himself, and downed the contents in two long shuddering swallows. "Oh, God!"

Two small hands settled on his shoulders from behind and tugged him against the back of the sofa. He groaned and let his head fall against the soft feminine swell of her belly as delicate fingers touched his temples, began gently, deftly stroking them.

Astonishingly, they seemed to ease all but the fiercest pounding and he let himself relax. Then, after a long while, he finally opened his eyes.

Closed them again a startled moment later. He leaned forward, resting his elbows on his knees again, eyes still closed. "Go away," he said thickly. "You're just a dream."

It happened, sometimes. Even without the bourbon. He couldn't count the number of times he'd thought he felt her beside him in the night, heard her soft laugh, caught a glimpse of flashing eyes and a mane of dark hair.

Funny, the tricks a man's mind played.

She wasn't a dream, of course. Just someone he'd found last night—or one of two or three last nights—and had brought home, someone dark-eyed and dark-haired and soft.

They always were. He'd bring them home and take them to bed and then, somewhere between the thinking about it and the actual act, he'd remember. He'd apologize and mumble something about being too tired to make it worth their while and send them home, unfulfilled and spitting mad, and he'd swear it was the last time.

Until the next time.

He swore softly, rubbing his face, a couple of days' growth of beard rasping against his fingers. He'd remember her name eventually. If he ever knew it. And, as with the others, he'd send her home. It was pointless not to. Pointless to pretend they could have anything between them but sex, and—as long as the memories haunted him—not particularly good sex at that.

He'd remember her name in a few minutes....

He started to stand up before he realized he was naked and, more for her sake than his, he draped the blanket around his hips and eased himself to his feet, groaning through clenched teeth. Then he turned unsteadily to look at his ministering angel.

She gazed back at him calmly. Her hair was a little shorter, maybe, but it was the same rich chocolate brown. She still wore it loose and straight, bangs glossy and square cut across her forehead, still had that way of looking at him, head tipped slightly, that made his throat go dry. Her mouth was still as rich and full-lipped as he remembered, her skin as porcelain-pale and perfect.

Only her eyes had changed. They were still wide and dark and thickly lashed, but they were filled with an infinite sadness that had never been there before, a weariness that he knew instinctively had been imbedded there for a long, long while.

"So it is you." His voice rasped, filled with accusation.

"Yes."

He nodded, immediately wished he hadn't as his stomach gave another unruly heave. "Am I supposed to say I'm glad to see you or something?"

A feathering of a smile brushed her mouth. "I don't expect that, no."

"Good." He turned his back on her and started to make his way toward the bathroom when, abruptly, he knew he wasn't going to make it.

He swore thickly and bolted for the front door, nearly tripping over Teddy. The dog leaped away with a yelp of surprise and Dev staggered down the steps and got as far as the front yard before his stomach betrayed him and he was violently and painfully sick.

Jess started after him out of habit, then caught herself and stayed where she was. He'd be all right. He'd just been drunk on cheap but honest bourbon, not revved up on liquor and pills, or coke or any of a hundred other chemical thrills. And, knowing Dev, he wouldn't appreciate having her witness his disgrace.

Teddy nudged the screen door open with his nose and came in, wagging his tail tentatively. Jess knelt beside him and stroked his muzzle and throat. "You haven't changed a bit, have you," she whispered. He nudged her hand with his wet nose, asking for more, and she smiled at him.

She could have sworn he remembered her. Did a dog's memories go back that far, she found herself wondering as she stroked his ears. It had been eight years since the last time he'd seen her. He'd been just a puppy back then, just two huge eyes and four huge feet and an appetite to match. Dev had found him in a roadside ditch during a pelting rainstorm and the two of them had come in about midnight, soaking wet and covered with mud and brambles and shivering with cold.

She'd given Dev a mug of hot buttered brandy and the pup a bowl of warm milk it had been too young to even lap properly. And as she'd watched Dev gently feed the tiny, shivering thing, she'd found herself filled with sudden jealousy at how easily he could show his love for an abandoned pup, and yet how impossibly hard it was for him to show that same love to her.

Teddy whimpered and Jess realized her fingers had tightened in the fur on his neck. She smiled faintly and gave him another pat, then got to her feet. Things had gotten complicated since that night eight years ago. A few weeks later she'd walked out of the apartment that she and Dev had been sharing for over a year, brokenhearted and pregnant with the child he didn't even know about. She'd married

Gary, and the rift between the two men had never healed. Then Gary had been killed and . . .

Jess looked around the room. And what? What *had* happened to Dev during those eight years? She'd kept track of him—it hadn't been hard, considering his career with the police department had been meteoric—but hearing it secondhand from Gary wasn't the same as hearing it from Dev himself.

She knew him too well for that. He was like deep still water, the unruffled surface mirroring calm reflections of what was going on around him while far below, hidden from everyone, lay the great whirlpools and riptides that were the real Devlin McAllister: compelling, mysterious, often deadly to any unsuspecting heart that ventured too near.

But after Gary had died two years ago, things had changed. There had been a case that had gone bad, a woman and her child who had died . . . an investigation afterward with accusations flying like chafe. Then Dev had resigned from the force and had become next thing to a recluse, cut off from civilization and everything it meant, making his living as a carpenter and repairman.

"Mo-o-om!" Heather's voice fluted in through the door from the kitchen. She followed it a moment later, eyes glowing. "There's a beach and everything! Can I—oh." Her gaze fell to the empty sofa and she sobered instantly. "Is *he* up?"

Jess saw the disgust on the small face, knew she was thinking of Gary. Of the drinking, the hangovers. "Yes," she said quietly. "He's up."

"He was drunk last night, wasn't he." It was more accusation than question.

"Yes," Jess repeated even more quietly, seeing no point in lying. Heather had been sound asleep when they'd arrived late last night, curled up in a blanket on the back seat of the rental car. Exhausted by the long boat ride over, she hadn't even wakened when Jess had carried her in and put her to bed in one of the spare rooms.

But she'd seen Dev on the sofa this morning; had seen the gaunt, unshaven face, the pile of wet, filthy clothes still lying on the bathroom floor. Knew—too well for a seven-year-old—what they meant.

"Is he going to be like this all the time?"

"I...don't know," Jess said quite truthfully. She'd wondered that herself more than once during the long, empty night, watching over him. Had wondered if the letter she'd found from Laurel Conroy's parents—the letter she'd shamelessly read—had been a trigger, or merely an excuse. "I hope not."

"Me too," Heather said with feeling. "Can I take Teddy down to the beach?"

Jess hesitated, then nodded. It might be easier, for now, to take this one step at a time. And Dev wasn't in any kind of shape right now to handle *this,* too. "Just be careful, Heather. And no talking to strangers, remember."

"I won't. Come on, Teddy!" The two of them headed through the kitchen at a dead run. The back door slammed open, then closed again with a bang, and Jess listened to Teddy's excited barking fade into the distance.

She walked across to the door, and looked out. Dev was sitting on the patch of threadbare grass that passed for a lawn, arms draped across his upraised knees, forehead resting on one clenched fist.

Pushing the screen door open, she stepped out onto the wide veranda and Dev glanced up, wincing slightly. He managed a droll smile, then eased himself onto his back, one arm thrown across his eyes. "Not a pretty sight, huh?"

"I've seen prettier." *And dealt with worse,* she added to herself. Gary's excursions into the no-man's-land of recreational drugs and liquor made Dev's brief dalliance look like child's play.

She leaned against one of the peeled pine posts supporting the railing and gazed down at him, trying to decipher the tangle of emotions she felt at seeing him again. She'd spent eight years wondering what she'd ever say if she met him face-to-face again. Eight years torn between love and anger, bitterness and regret.

But she'd grown up a lot over those eight years, understood things now she hadn't before, and the desperate need to strike out and hurt him as he'd hurt her seemed very far away. The overwhelming sensation she felt at this moment was one of weary sadness. Sadness for him, for the years they'd wasted, for all they'd put each other through.

Dev sat up again, slowly. His color had come back and although he was tousled and unshaven and decidedly worse for wear, it gave him an air of reckless disrepute that, on him, managed to look almost appealing. He had the kind of face that could handle a weekend drunk, as handsome as sin itself in that hard-hewn, slightly worn-around-the-edges way of a man who's been around.

His features were still straight and even, holding enough imperfections to be interesting, his jaw almost pugnaciously wide, his nose bearing the unmistakable signs of having been broken a time or two. It was the kind of face that would have been equally at home in a corporate boardroom or under a wide-brimmed, dusty Stetson or an oil rigger's hard hat or staring narrow-eyed through the spray at the helm of a big square-rigger as she fought her way around the Horn.

He looked up just then. His eyes met hers head-on for the first time since she'd gotten here and Jess went very still. But there was none of the anger or antagonism that she'd half expected. He looked faintly bemused, as though still only half-convinced that she was real and not some dream image conjured out of bad whiskey and too many sleepless nights. For a split second she could have sworn she saw his gaze gentle as he looked at her, saw something that in any other man might have been wistfulness. But then it was gone.

For some reason, it nearly made her smile. Same old Dev. He'd always been a master of hiding what he was thinking and feeling, even from her. She couldn't count the number of times she'd watched that mask come down and had known he'd shut her out again and had felt the ache in her heart cut a little deeper.

"How did you find me?" His voice was just a rasp.

"Mary."

He gave a grunt and Jess smiled dryly. "She worries about you."

"Like hell." He rubbed his hands over his stubbled cheeks wearily. "She's never given a damn before. Why should she start now?"

"She *is* your sister. I guess, for her, anyway, that counts for something."

Dev gave a snort and eased himself to his feet, the blanket draped precariously around his midsection. "Not in our family, sweetheart. The only thing that held us together was fear, and when the old man finally killed himself we didn't even have that anymore. And besides, she'd left long before that."

So, the hurt was still there. All these years and he was still bitter about the way Mary had left when the leaving was good, abandoning her four younger siblings to the vague, dreamlike woman who was their mother and their drunken tyrant of a father. She'd been the only person who had been able to keep Bud McAllister under control, her own fiery temper matching his outburst for outburst, but when she'd left, there had been no buffer between him and the children he bullied relentlessly.

Dev had been twelve that summer. And the ongoing battle between he and his father had taken a turn for the worst. It had continued for thirteen more years, and by the time it was over, Dev had been marked for life.

"Would you like me to fix you some breakfast?"

"God, no." Dev shuddered as he walked by her without so much as a glance. He strode up the steps and into the house, letting the screen door bang closed behind him.

Jess caught the lightning flash of anger as it flickered through her. She'd known it was going to be like this, she reminded herself.

But had she, really? Or had she managed to convince herself, at some deep-down level, that he'd be as glad to see her as she was him? It was that part of her that Dev had always laughed at, the romantic posies-and-lace part of her that had kept her in his bed long after common sense had told her to leave, that had filled her with the hope that he'd actually marry her one day.

She smiled faintly, and followed him inside.

Dev ran the sink full of ice water and buried his face in it. He held it there for as long as he could, then reared back and shook himself like a dog, spraying water. Hands braced on either side of the sink, he stood there for a moment or two, and then, slowly, lifted his head and met his own eyes in the mirror.

What he saw made him wince. Two sunken, bloodshot eyes glowered back at him accusingly and his cheeks, under the stubble, were pale and sallow. There was a good-sized bruise on his left temple and he fingered it curiously, wincing again, and it was only then that he realized his left hand was bandaged. The gauze and tape were smeared with dirt and blood and he flexed his hand cautiously, relieved to find it stiff and sore but seemingly undamaged.

What the hell had he been doing these past . . . how many days? Two? Three? He had a dim recollection of running out of bourbon and setting out for town to buy more, but after that things got hazy. There'd been a woman...at least he thought there had been a woman. Maybe he'd just dreamed her. Like Jess. She *had* to be just a dream.

It wouldn't be the first time.

Except that she *was* real this time, he reminded himself brutally. It hadn't been his imagination; she really was here.

Had he phoned her? He couldn't imagine being *that* drunk, but hell, a man did strange things sometimes after he'd been swimming around in the bottom of a bottle of bourbon for a few days. He'd gotten a letter, he remembered that. And a package. . . .

He remembered then, with vivid clarity. His stomach gave
a sharp twist and he swore, letting his head hang limply between his outstretched arms, eyes closed, cold water drip-
dripping from his hair into the sink.

The bracelet. That damned bracelet. Just when he'd
started to get over it. Almost, anyway. Some nights he was
able to sleep right through without being ambushed by the
nightmares. Without waking up screaming into the darkness, seeing it happening all over again. Seeing the bodies,
the blood . . .

He swore again, violently this time, and shoved himself
upright.

How long she'd been standing there behind him, watching, he had no idea. Jess's eyes met his in the mirror above
the sink, filled with a pain he knew instinctively was for him.
It annoyed him for some reason. He held her gaze deliberately, daring her to say anything, and after a moment she
frowned and looked down.

Still not meeting his eyes, she set a glass of orange juice
on the vanity. "This might help. And when you come
downstairs, I'll put a clean dressing on your hand."

So that's where the bandage had come from. He flexed his
fingers, then looked up to meet her gaze in the mirror again.
"How did I do it?"

A smile may have brushed her mouth, gone before he
could be sure. "You were carrying a bottle of bourbon when
you fell. It broke."

"Fell?" He frowned, trying to remember.

"In the ditch. Out by the gate . . . don't you remember?"

Dev managed a grim smile. "Sweetheart, all I remember
is reaching for that damned bottle a few days ago. The rest
is blank." He clenched his fist another time or two, frowning. "What was I doing out by the gate?"

"Running your truck into it, mainly."

"Truck?" He winced again. "Was I coming or going?"

"Going. Except you didn't make it past the gatepost, thank heaven. I guess you got out to look at the damage and slipped in the mud."

"Without even dropping the bottle," he said wryly.

Another smile brushed her mouth. "If it hadn't broken, you wouldn't have spilled a drop."

He nodded slowly. Thoughtfully. "So it *was* you." His eyes captured hers on glass. "I thought I'd dreamt it."

"No." She held his gaze. "I found you out there and brought you in. Got you cleaned up as best I could."

"You...uh...handle this kind of thing pretty well."

She frowned very faintly. "Let's just say I've had some experience handling drunks with attitude."

"And...the shower?"

He'd have missed it if he hadn't known her so damned well. She'd never been able to lie to him, and in some perverse way it pleased him to discover he could still catch the telltale clues: the hint of color in her cheeks, the tiny frown between her brows, gone almost as quickly as it formed, the way she let her eyes slide from his. He found himself staring at her reflection and taunted himself with the memory of how she'd felt in his hands, wet and slippery and warm. And real. As real as she'd been eight years ago....

She glanced up again and caught him watching her. She held his stare with a defiance he found almost touching, and he suddenly realized that a hell of a lot of what had happened in that shower last night had been as real as the two of them standing here this morning.

He could hurt her, he realized with chilling clarity. All it would take would be a couple of well-chosen words, and that defiance would crumple and vanish, leaving her as vulnerable as a fawn to the poacher's gun.

But the temptation was gone almost as quickly as it swept over him, leaving him feeling a little sick. There was no sport in hurting her. Never had been. She'd always been too trusting, too open, and whenever he'd given in to the urge to hurt her, he'd hated himself afterward. He'd never even known why he'd done it half the time, except to drive her off whenever she got too close. And maybe that's all it had been, he found himself musing. Maybe that's what it had all been about....

He gave himself a mental shake and reached for the can of shaving foam. He'd probably cut his throat, the way his hands were shaking, but even the thought of using the electric razor made his teeth ache. "I'll be down as soon as I clean up," he growled, not looking at her. And a moment later, she was gone.

Two

She found the bracelet when she started tidying up the living room.

It had fallen under the edge of the coffee table. She'd seen a glitter of something gold and had knelt down to retrieve it, exclaiming gently when she realized what it was.

He still had it. Even after all these years. All that had happened...

For some reason it brought a prickle of unexpected tears to her eyes as she ran the links through her fingers. She'd given it to him the same night she'd told him for the first time that she loved him. The night she'd broken her own promise to herself and agreed to move in with him. And much later that same night, gazing into his eyes as he'd made slow, gentle love to her, she'd known that things were going to work out after all.

Jess smiled to herself again. And it had. For a while, at least. Until her need for marriage and security had collided head-on with Dev's need to be free.

The memories made her frown slightly and she folded her
fingers around the bracelet, her throat aching suddenly with
tears she'd thought she'd shed long ago. There was a framed
photograph lying just under the coffee table and she looked
at it for a long while, then bent down and picked it up.

The glass was broken, as though from a sharp blow. Or a
boot heel, she mused grimly. From what she'd seen, Dev
hadn't been in any shape for fond reminiscing these past few
days.

She stared thoughtfully at it. Like the ID bracelet, it was
part of a past long gone. A past she'd thought he had re-
jected years ago. It surprised her slightly to find he'd kept
the photograph.

It was of the three of them—Dev, Gary and her—arms
linked, laughing happily and mugging for the camera. She
was in the middle, as always, looking happy and relaxed.
She'd never noticed until now how Dev had slipped his arm
around her waist and had tugged her against him so in that
instant she was standing nearer to him than to Gary. He was
looking straight into the camera with that lazy, self-
confident smile, as though to tell anyone who happened by
that she and the world were his and his alone.

Then her gaze moved to Gary, and she smiled a little. His
oak-brown hair was wind-tousled and he was laughing, teeth
glinting in the sunlight, and he had his arm draped almost
protectively around her shoulders. His eyes seemed to hold
hers and she found herself thinking of the first time he'd
told her he loved her. Of how, if she insisted on staying with
Dev, she was only going to be hurt.

"He can't love you, Jessie," he'd shouted at her angrily
that afternoon. "Damn it, he can't love anyone, can't you
see that? He's too closed off for that. He'll just break your
heart, Jess. And I might not be there to pick up the pieces!"

He had been, of course. Gary had always been there to
pick up the pieces. He'd married her when Dev wouldn't,
had raised Dev's daughter as his, had held her in the night
when she'd wept for Dev's touch.

Except he'd gotten lost somewhere along the way. The Gary she'd married hadn't been the one she'd grown up with. He had been a stranger, looking at her through Gary's eyes. She'd left finally, taking her broken dreams and her daughter with her. Two years later he was dead, the stranger he'd become finally put to rest.

She didn't even know what made her look up in that instant. Dev was standing in the doorway leading from the kitchen, leaning against the frame as though he'd been there for a while, watching her. His eyes were thoughtful, almost pensive, and he held her gaze wordlessly. And in that heartbeat of time, Jess knew they'd been sharing the same thoughts, the same memories. Perhaps even the same regrets.

She smiled faintly and looked back down at the photo. "Do you remember when Gary took this? You'd given him that new camera for his birthday, and he'd been dying to use the self-timer...."

She hadn't heard him move, didn't know he'd crossed the room until a strong, sun-browned hand reached down and took the picture from her almost gently. "You'll cut yourself," he said gruffly. "It must have fallen."

Jess found herself suddenly blinking back tears. "What happened to us, Dev?" she whispered. "We were so happy then."

He was silent for a long moment. "We grew up," he growled finally, tossing the photograph onto the coffee table. "Life got real."

She nodded, getting to her feet wearily, and looked up to discover that he was staring at her again. He was leaning against the wide mantle, one boot-clad foot resting on the raised hearth, his expression closed and private.

His eyes locked with hers and Jess felt her heart give a distinct cartwheel, her mouth going suddenly dry. There was a long silent while when neither of them spoke, then Jess finally managed a rough gasp of laughter. "I wish you'd say something, Dev. The suspense is killing me."

To her relief, a very faint smile brushed his mouth. He nodded slowly and let his gaze drift almost idly over her. It was a thorough gaze, done deliberately, she suspected, to get a rise out of her.

But she was damned if she'd give him the satisfaction. Not moving so much as a hair, she simply stood there and took it. And when his eyes finally met hers again, she held them defiantly. "Well?"

Again, that faint smile lifted one corner of his mouth. "You're looking good, Jess. Damned good."

"Too bad I can't say the same for you."

Dev gave a snort of laughter and shrugged away from the fireplace. He'd deserved that. "You didn't exactly catch me at my best," he drawled.

Eight years, he found himself musing. It was hard to believe it had been that long. He could still remember the taste of her, like a rare good wine sampled once but never forgotten. And the feel of her all around him in the night. Damn it, all he had to do was close his eyes and—

"I hope this didn't have anything to do with... well, with the state you were in when I found you."

Dev glanced around, his stomach pulling tight when he saw the bracelet dangling from her fingers. His lip curled slightly. "Don't flatter yourself, sweetheart." He strolled across to where she was standing, taking grim satisfaction in seeing her flinch slightly when he took the bracelet roughly from her fingers. He looked at it for a moment, then tossed it carelessly onto the table beside the photograph. "I got over you long ago."

"I never meant to hurt you, Dev," she whispered.

"You didn't hurt me." He turned his head to look at her, feeling old anger claw at his insides like something wanting out. "Like I said, don't flatter yourself."

She glanced up, her eyes filled with pain. "I don't deserve this, Dev. It wasn't all my fault. You were as much to blame as I was."

"Yeah?" He gave another snort and walked across to the fireplace, flexing his left hand where he'd cut it with the broken bottle. "Funny, I don't remember that part. All I remember was coming back to the apartment and finding you gone. Then going over to Elliott's and finding the two of you there, all wrapped up in each other."

"That wasn't the way it happened, and you know it. You walked out on me, remember, not the other way around. Just like you always walked out when the words *marriage* or *commitment* or *love* came up."

It stung, as she'd likely meant it to, and Dev felt a jolt of instinctive anger. "Bull! We had an argument that night— hell, we spent half our time together arguing about one thing or another! I went out to walk around the block a few times to cool off, and when I got back you were gone." He strode across to where she was standing. "*You* walked out on *me,* lady," he reminded her angrily, jabbing his finger at her for emphasis.

To his surprise, she didn't back down as she would have eight years ago. Instead, hands planted on slim hips, she actually took a step toward him and glared up at him.

"Don't you try to bully me, McAllister. And don't you dare try to lay what happened at *my* feet! When you went storming out that night, you were angrier than I'd ever seen you. I didn't know if I was ever going to see you again. And Gary was there for me. Just like he was *always* there for me when I needed him."

The way you weren't, the unspoken censure in her voice added. As it always did, hearing Gary's name, thinking of him, sent a shaft of pain twisting through Dev's gut. He had the sudden image of a dark windswept wharf, of Gary's face in the moonlight, wearing that familiar cocky, didn't-give-a-damn expression, the fear and shame in his eyes . . . the sound of that gunshot . . .

He shrugged it off. "He had a hell of a unique way of providing sympathy," he said bitterly.

"He was trying to comfort me," Jess said quietly. Maybe too quietly. There was a glitter in her eyes that could only be called dangerous.

"I guess that's one way of putting it." Dev stared down at her deliberately. "I always wondered something, Jess—how many other times had Gary *been* there when you and I had an argument? I figure in those last few months alone you must have spent damned near as much time in his bed as in mine."

She moved so fast that had his instincts been half a heartbeat slower, she'd have practically taken his head off with the swing she took at him. But even hung over, he was faster. He caught her wrist before her open-palmed blow could connect and he held it firmly, watching the fury in her eyes turn to outrage, watching her fight the temptation to come at him with everything she had.

To his satisfaction she didn't. She eased a long, tight breath between her teeth and subsided, and when he relaxed his grip she wrenched her wrist out of his hand and backed off a few steps, breathing heavily, her eyes almost black with anger. "Damn you, Devlin," she said in a harsh undertone.

It was a small victory. And one he found himself almost regretting. Hell, maybe she deserved one free shot at him. Maybe he owed her that much.

But he wasn't ready to concede quite yet; those old wounds were still a little too painful. "He sure as hell didn't waste any time laying his claim after I was out of the picture, did he?"

Something shifted deep in Jess's dark eyes and she hesitated, then let her gaze slip from his. Almost guiltily, Dev found himself thinking. But then she met his eyes again, and whatever emotion he'd seen for that split second was gone.

"You could have laid your own claim if you'd wanted it badly enough," she reminded him pointedly. "I lived with you for a year and a half—and it was you who wanted it that way, not me. I wanted marriage, remember? And kids, and . . . and all the rest."

There it was again: the slight hesitation, the glance down, the faint frown. And, again, she seemed to shake it off. When they met his again, her eyes were defiant. "I loved you so much I was crazy with it. Gary was my friend, but you were the one I loved."

"And Gary was the one you married."

The words hung between them, as rank as smoke.

"Because I had—" She stopped, cheeks flushed, eyes snapping with anger and old pain. She hugged herself suddenly and wheeled away from him, silken hair cascading around her shoulders. "I had my reasons," she said in a half whisper.

"You knew how I felt about marriage before you moved in with me," he reminded her angrily.

"And you knew how I felt before you asked!" She gave her head a toss and looked around at him, dark eyes flashing. "My mother wasted her entire life waiting for that *bastard*—my father—to marry her. He had his wife and his kids and his big house, and yet my mother actually believed his lies. Believed he'd give up all that to marry her.

"So she waited. Year after year, living in that dingy little house on Hazelton, surviving on the crumbs of hope he'd toss her. She loved him so much she was blind to everything—she just sat by the phone day in and day out, dreaming of when he'd leave his wife and everything would be perfect!"

Her voice cracked slightly and she wheeled away, back stiff. "He'd drop by every couple of weeks to *visit,* and I can still remember that pathetic look of hope and expectation on her face when he'd drive up in that big car. He'd spend his hour or two with her, then he'd leave and go home to his wife and his children, and I'd listen to her crying half the night. . . ."

Dev said nothing. He remembered. Remembered seeing the big silver Mercedes in the driveway of Jess's house every couple of weeks and knowing he'd find her huddled in the tree house, dirty cheeks tracked with tears of shame and fury. He'd think up some game to distract her and soon he'd have her laughing again, but underneath the laughter lay a desperate need for security and love and family that he'd never really understood until years later. But by then she was already in love with him and it was too late.

"My leaving was inevitable, Dev. It just happened a little sooner than you were prepared for, that's all." She turned around, her smile bitter. "That's why you were so angry with Gary and me—not that I'd left, but that I'd called your bluff when you weren't expecting it and caught you by surprise."

Dev managed a harsh laugh as she turned away and walked back toward the fireplace. "I guess we'll never know."

"Oh, I think we do," Jess said softly. "I think we do, Dev."

Dev caught his reply and swallowed it, some of his anger dissipating before he could stop it. Hell, she was half right. More than half, probably.

He'd wanted her, but not the marriage he knew was only a trap, had cajoled and sweet-talked her into moving in with him even while knowing she was far from happy with it. She'd expected him to marry her, he'd known that from the start, but he'd convinced himself that she'd get over it once she realized how happy they could be without it.

Except she hadn't. Marriage had been more than just a word to Jess. Marriage meant *family,* and family was the one thing she'd never had.

Dev smiled bitterly. And family had always been the one thing he'd had too damned much of. He'd watched his parents' marriage dissolve into open warfare over the years, had listened to the screaming, the fights, the violence. Had watched his mother turn bitter and ugly with resentment and his father sink deeper and deeper into the sullen anger and whiskey-fueled rages that had turned the house on Hazelton into a battleground.

He found himself gazing at her, half wanting to take the few steps separating them and slip his arms around her. She'd filled out a bit since he'd seen her last, her trim little body still slender but with a hint of feminine lushness to her hips and breasts that hadn't been there before, and he knew exactly how she'd feel against him. Could remember exactly what it had been like to pull her down across him and lose himself in her, to feel her respond to his lovemaking with every cell of her body until she'd be half-crazy with it, begging him for more.

His own body responded with a vigor that caught him by surprise and he swore under his breath, angered at how easy it was to forget the hurt. It shouldn't be easy. Not the kind of hell she'd put him through!

He was standing behind her, so close that Jess swore she could feel his breath stir her hair. All he'd have to do was touch her, and she'd lose it. So far she'd managed to hang onto her calm facade, but it was wearing very thin very fast. One touch, and it would shatter like the glass in that photograph.

The silence stretched, pulling so tight the air in the room all but hummed with it. She could hear him shift restlessly, could feel his stare burning into her back. Everything they hadn't yet said hung between them like war flags and Jess found herself wondering desperately how she'd ever convinced herself it was going to be easy. That after eight years, Devlin McAllister had forgiven her.

She should have known better. Damn it, she should have known! "Say something." She swallowed a sob of laughter.

"What the hell do you want me to say, Jess?" he asked with quiet savagery. "That I hate waking up every morning of my life because it means facing another day without you? That there hasn't been a night in eight years that I haven't dreamed of you? A woman I didn't pretend was you?" His fingers gripped her arms and Jess flinched.

His breath curled around the side of her throat, warm and moist, and she froze. "Do you want me to tell you that just seeing you here brings it all back?" he whispered ferociously, his mouth against her ear. "That hangover or no hangover, I'd like to strip you out of those jeans and lay you down on this rug and—"

"Mommy!" The voice came floating through the screen door, disembodied and breathless, and Jess felt Dev stiffen. Footsteps pounded across the veranda, accompanied by the patter of clawed paws, and an instant later the screen door banged open and Heather and Teddy came flying into the room. "Mommy, someone's coming!" Heather saw Dev just then and careened to a stop, eyes widening, her mouth a small round O of shock.

Dev released her so abruptly that Jess had to take a step to catch her balance. She drew in a deep, unsteady breath. "Heather, this is Mr. McAllister—in a little better condition than when you saw him earlier." Swallowing, Jess turned to face Dev. It was hard, meeting his eyes. But she did it. "Dev, this is my daughter, Heather."

Dev's eyes were still dark with anger and some other, fiercer emotion that Jess didn't even want to think about. He held her gaze for one vibrant moment, then eased his breath between clenched teeth and nodded at Heather, relaxing.

"Someone's coming," Heather repeated nervously.

"Is it the same car?" Jess tried to keep her voice casual, as much to keep Heather calm as to allay Dev's suspicions, but she failed miserably, was aware of the speculative way he looked at her.

"I don't think so."

Jess looked at Dev, her smile stiff. "Expecting company?"

"No." He said it abruptly, his hard look telling her more clearly than words that most people knew enough to leave him in peace. Then, almost grudgingly, he added, "But I know who it is."

Heather had inched her way around the big platform rocker by the fireplace and was standing there now, clearly frightened, and Jess walked over to give her a reassuring hug. "It's all right, honey," she said quietly. "He didn't follow us here. He has no idea where we are...none at all."

Heather nodded stiffly, obviously unconvinced, and Teddy whimpered, sensing her fear.

Watching Frankie Hudson's beat-up old truck come bouncing and rattling down the lane, Dev struggled to get his rampaging anger under some sort of control. It was an all-encompassing sort of anger, coming out of nowhere. He supposed it had been down there inside him for years, festering away, but it had caught him by surprise.

And under the anger were a whole lot of other feelings he hadn't counted on: need, want, regret, all of them tangled up with the dark-eyed woman he'd thought he would never see again.

Damn it, what had brought her back into his life!

He glanced around at her and the girl, another kind of anger flirting through him now. *Spit it out, lady,* he told her silently. What are you running away from? And why here? Why me?

The girl—Heather—was watching him uneasily, and Dev found himself staring at her, feeling a sudden jolt of déjà vu. It took him a moment to figure out why, and when he remembered he very nearly smiled.

Jessie! She was the spitting image of Jess the first time he'd seen her, hair all atangle, small face smudged with dirt, defiant and scared to death all at the same time.

He'd been twelve the summer that she and her mother had moved into the run-down little house next door. His father had been drinking more than usual and Dev had taken to spending more and more time in the big tree house in the huge old oak in Jess's backyard.

That tree house had always been his. The woman who had owned the house before Jess's mother hadn't cared. She'd been well into her sixties, the tree house built by some son long grown and gone, and she'd seemed happy that it was being used again. It had been his secret place—his retreat—since he'd been old enough to climb, and he'd been fully prepared to fight for his territorial rights before Jess and her mother had even finished unpacking.

The foliage had been so thick that it had taken Jess nearly a week to even realize that the huge oak in her new backyard harbored a tree house. And another couple of days to work up the courage to climb that high to reach it. But when she'd finally decided to do it, she'd shinnied up the tree like a monkey, laughing with delight at her discovery.

Only to find that her hard-won conquest was already occupied. She'd stared at Dev in much the same way Heather was staring at him now, her chin tilted at the same stubborn angle, mouth set with determination. They'd traded a few hostile words over ownership, Dev calmly pointing out that the tree might be growing in *her* backyard but that he had about seven years of squatter's rights on his side. Not to mention the fact that he and his best friend, Gary Elliott, were more than a match for any scrawny if pugnacious seven-year-old girl.

Their first confrontation had ended in a standoff. Their second, a few days later, had resulted in an uneasy alliance. And by the end of the next week, all three were fast friends.

God, how easy it had been back then, Dev found himself musing. Almost as easy as falling in love had been . . .

He caught his rambling thoughts and shook them off impatiently. Frankie Hudson had parked her old truck and was walking toward the house. He held the screen door for her. "You're looking good today, Frankie."

The figure that strode into the living room responded with a succinct barnyard epithet, eyeing Dev suspiciously on the way by. "Surprised to see you sober. Run outa whiskey?"

It took Jess a moment to realize that Dev's visitor was a woman. She was wearing a pair of men's denim coveralls, the legs stuffed into tall rubber boots, and a searing pink shirt that sported green and orange pineapples. She'd stuffed her gray hair under a peak cap that sported the logo for a well-known brewery, and as she stamped into the middle of the room, she fastened one sharp eye on Jess.

"Got yerself a lady friend, do you?" she said with a sly look in Dev's direction. Her weathered face split into an engaging smile and she strode over to Jess, wiping her hand on her coveralls before extending it. "Name's Frances Hudson—everyone calls me Frankie."

Smiling, Jess took Frankie's hand. "I'm Jess, an old friend of Dev's."

"You don't say." Those bright blue eyes wandered over Jess with disturbing thoroughness. "City gal, are ya?"

Jess had to laugh. "That obvious, is it?"

"Mrs. Elliott is from Seattle," Dev put in, stressing the *Mrs.* just slightly. "How much do I owe you for the—?"

"Stayin' awhile, or just visitin'?"

"Just visiting," Jess lied smoothly. "Dev and I grew up together. We've just been catching up on...old times." She could feel Dev's gaze boring into her, but refused to look at him.

Frankie nodded again, giving Dev a glance. "Good. Not healthy for a man to spend all his time alone."

"How much do I owe you for that lumber?" Dev repeated testily.

"Don't worry about it. I need'ja to come over an' fix them danged steps up to my place anyway. Stove's broke again, too."

"I'll get over there later this week."

Frankie spotted Heather just then. "Well, well, who's this?"

"My daughter, Heather," Jess said.

"Really." Those shrewd blue eyes rested briefly on Heather. "Nice-looking girl, *Mrs*. Jess Elliott. Mighty nice looking. Got a lot of her father in 'er, would you say?"

Jess's heart gave a thump, but she managed to hold Frankie's gaze without flinching. "Yes," she said very calmly. "She does."

Frankie gave a thoughtful nod, casting a speculative glance at Dev. "You give any more thought to running for Tulley's job when he retires next month?"

"Not interested," Dev replied succinctly.

"Tulley seems to think you'd make a crackerjack chief of police," Frankie persisted. "So do most folks hereabouts."

"I said I'm not interested." Dev's voice held a distinct edge, but it didn't seem to faze Frankie.

She just smiled blandly at him. "You won't get no competition from nobody I can think of. Tulley won't run again—he's too damn old and fat, and lazier 'n a house cat besides."

"That bilge pump you wanted repaired is out back," Dev said in a dangerously quiet voice, heading for the door. "It needed cleaning and a new set of gaskets. I'll give you a hand getting it in the truck."

He stalked out without so much as a backward glance. Frankie followed a moment later, then Heather called Teddy and went bounding back outside, fears forgotten, and Jess discovered she was alone. She eased her breath out, still feeling a little shaken, and rubbed her upper arms where Dev's fingers had dug into her.

So. She hadn't been the only one harboring a lot of memories and hurt for these past eight years. She'd expected to come out here and find the same old Dev—self-confident and maybe a little cool, a little distant. But this Devlin McAllister was . . . different.

In spite of herself, Jess had to smile. Of course he was different—eight years different. Just as she was. Eight years ago she'd been a college kid of twenty-one, pregnant, scared to death and filled with shame. She'd been so much in love she'd been blinded by it, and—frantic not to repeat the mistake her own mother had made—she'd grabbed the first way out she was offered. Gary's way.

Which had been a mistake fully as great as her mother's—just different.

Jess walked across and started straightening up the cushions on the sofa where Dev had spent the night. Gathering up the pillow and sheets, she set them aside and adjusted the sofa cushions, then sat on the big hassock with a weary sigh.

Maybe it had been a mistake coming out here. Somehow she'd convinced herself that Dev would be there for her when she needed him, just as he had when they'd been kids.

He'd been her knight-errant back then, strong and wise and patient, as all good knights should be. He routinely made short work of any neighborhood kid reckless enough to taunt her about her father, and on those occasions when it happened anyway he'd wipe the tears from her eyes and comfort her, just like best friends were supposed to.

And if Dev wasn't there, Gary was. Best friends. Comrades-in-arms. One for all, and all for one. . . .

Idly, Jess reached across and picked up the framed photograph that was still lying on the coffee table. The three of them looked so happy and alive and filled with expectation, the world theirs for the taking, and Jess found herself smiling in response.

That's exactly the way they'd been back then—hopeful and reckless and innocent of what was to come. She'd loved both of them and they'd loved her back with that tolerant, teasing big-brother kind of love that was only just starting to turn into something else.

Jess sighed. They'd had no idea, those three laughing people, of the storm lurking on their horizon. A few months after the picture was taken, Dev and Gary had had their first serious fight, a bare-knuckled brawl that had left them both bleeding and sullen with anger.

It had been over her, of course. The first of many. They'd made up not long afterward, laughing about it and punching each other playfully on the shoulder, gruff and embarrassed, pretending it had been nothing. And yet it had been. They'd all sensed it.

Something had changed that summer. Dev and Gary had come home from college and suddenly they'd been next thing to adults, standing tall and handsome in the sunlight, young men instead of the boys who'd hugged her goodbye only months earlier. She'd changed, too, of course. But she hadn't realized how much until Dev had looked at her when he'd gotten off the plane and she'd seen something in his eyes that had never been there before.

He'd looked at her that day the way a man looks at a woman, and even then, in some dim, instinctual way, she'd sensed that things would never be the same between them. She remembered that she'd blushed, suddenly flustered, and that he'd laughed and had swept her up in a ferocious hug, recalled the roughness of his unshaven cheek on hers and the realization in that moment that Dev—her Dev—wasn't a boy anymore.

The kiss he'd given her hadn't been the innocent kiss of a boy, either, she remembered. And the delicious shock that had run through her at the touch of his lips had left her breathless.

Damn. Jess drew in an unsteady breath, annoyed to discover how close she was to tears. They'd had it all back then. Or thought they had. How had things gone so wrong?

She put the picture back down, blinking hard, and picked up the ID bracelet, running the links through her fingers. More memories. More echoes of things best left unremembered.

It could have been only yesterday that she'd seen it lying on blue velvet in the jeweler's window. It had taken one look for her to know she had to get it for him. And one look at the price tag to know she couldn't afford it.

But she'd gone in anyway, and five minutes later she'd placed a pile of bills on the counter as a deposit. The money had been for textbooks for the next semester of college, but nothing was more important at that moment than the bracelet. She'd left it to be engraved, and when she'd picked it up a few days later any doubts had vanished.

She ran her thumb over the engraving idly, wondering why he'd kept it all these years.

Strange, the bits and pieces of the past one clung to. She still had the arrowheads he'd given her when she was eight, and the slingshot he'd made for her the following summer—the one that had gotten her soundly scolded after she'd put a sizable rock through Judge Hammond's sitting room window. It had been Dev and Gary who had dared her to do it, of course. Even then, she'd have walked through fire if either of them had asked.

Still would, probably, she found herself musing. The question was, would Dev do the same for her?

One moment Dev was asleep and the next he was wide-awake, heart jackhammering against his ribs, every nerve taut.

The house was dark and still. He could hear the leaves in the trees outside his window rustle as a light breeze fingered them, and, in the distance, the ever-present boom of the sea. Silently, he eased himself from beneath the covers and padded across to the window, eyes narrowing as he scanned the moonlit yard, the dark rim of forest beyond.

Nothing.

It may have been a dream. It wouldn't be the first time he'd awakened all tangled up in a nightmare, battling things that left him shaking for hours afterward. There were some nights he didn't go to bed at all, knowing they were waiting there for him in the dark corners of his mind, waiting to ambush him the moment he relaxed his vigilance.

He swore under his breath and shrugged his shoulders, trying to ease the tension across them as he turned away from the window. There was nothing out there. Teddy would be barking up a storm if there were. Whatever had wakened him was no more than imagination and bad nerves.

He scrubbed his fingers through his tousled hair. There was no point in going back to bed. Restless and edgy and wide-awake, he'd just lie there staring at the ceiling thinking about things he'd rather not.

Like the dark-eyed woman asleep in the guest room just down the corridor, for instance.

Frowning, he started rummaging through the drawers in the dresser. He had no idea why he'd asked her to stay. He'd been living out here alone for over a year now, sharing his life and living space with no one but Teddy, and he liked it that way. But when the time had come for Jess to leave that evening, he'd heard himself gruffly telling her that she and the kid could spend the night.

Not finding what he was looking for, he opened the closet and poked through the clutter on the shelf, then started looking through the two cardboard cartons on the floor.

For some reason he still couldn't quite pin down it had seemed important to keep her there. Part of it was a sense of unfinished business—the awareness that they'd left more unsaid today than said. But there was something else, too. Something about the fear in her eyes when Frankie Hudson had come in, the way she kept glancing nervously up the lane when she thought he wouldn't notice, the way she jumped at every noise and sudden movement.

Something was frightening her. Something bad enough to make her come to him—the last person on earth he'd have expected her to turn to.

Which was undoubtedly why, he advised himself irritably, he was prowling around his own house at two in the morning looking for his damned gun.

He pulled his jeans on finally and silently made his way down to the kitchen. The revolver was where he'd hidden it, stashed in a small locked cashbox on the highest shelf of the pantry, right behind two empty bourbon bottles.

Pulling the box down, he opened it. He took the revolver out and loaded it, fighting a superstitious little shiver. He hadn't had the thing out of the box in the year he'd moved out here. Hadn't fired any weapon since that day fifteen months ago when he'd brought Martin Conroy down with one fatal shot from his service revolver. Had sworn he'd never fire another...

He shook the memories off and checked the weapon expertly. Odds were he wouldn't need it, but it wouldn't hurt to have it handy. Then, knowing there was no reason for it but unable to help himself, he started checking the house.

Not bothering to turn the lights on, he padded soundlessly from room to room, but everything was as it should be—doors locked, windows secured. Whatever had wakened him had either gone, or had never existed in the first place.

It wouldn't be the first time that had happened, either. He shoved the revolver into the back waistband of his jeans and wandered down to the kitchen, trying to shake off an uneasy little prickle of suspicion. Instinct. It had kept him alive on more than one occasion, and he'd learned to listen to it. That, and the small cold spot between his shoulder blades. Although what it meant now was anyone's guess....

What it was that made him stop at the door of the kitchen, he had no idea. But suddenly he knew—without even knowing how—that he wasn't alone. The muscles in his belly pulled tight as he stepped soundlessly into the darkened room.

Her back was to him. She'd opened the fridge and was standing there thoughtfully gazing at the contents, barefooted and tousle-haired, silhouetted perfectly against the light. Whatever she was wearing didn't amount to much, backlit like that, and Dev could see the curve of waist and hip and long, smooth thigh through the filmy stuff of her nightclothes.

She reached forward to take something out and her breasts were suddenly outlined against the light, lush and unrestrained. And Dev found himself remembering the sweet weight of them in his hands, how the full dark tips would pucker when he took them in his mouth.

He found himself thinking of other things, then: the expression in her eyes when he made love to her; looking across a room at a party and seeing her there and knowing she was his; the way she had of creating a tiny cocoon of calm and sanity in a world gone mad. Things he'd missed without even realizing it....

Three

Jess was just swinging the fridge door closed and turning toward the counter when she saw the tall, silent figure standing in the darkness near the door. She froze, the carton of milk still suspended above the counter, and then in the next instant she realized who it was and let her breath out in a huff of relief.

"I didn't hear you come in," she said carelessly, setting the milk firmly on the counter. Her heart was beating like a runaway flywheel and she drew in a deep breath, hoping he didn't see the stark terror on her face. "Can't sleep?"

"No better than you, apparently." His voice was as offhand as hers.

"I was going to warm some milk—that sometimes helps. Would you like a glass?"

"I'll pass."

She'd noticed the metal box lying open on the counter but hadn't thought anything of it until Dev eased it almost too casually toward him. Then it hit her. He'd always kept his service revolver in a box like that, locked and out of sight on the shelf of his closet.

Swallowing, she looked at him questioningly. His eyes held hers in the moon-grayed darkness, then he smiled very faintly and pulled a small handgun from his waistband and casually emptied the cylinder, tossing it and the bullets into the box. "I thought I heard something," he said even more casually.

"Oh?" She tried to sound as unconcerned as he, but her voice cracked slightly.

"It must have been the wind. Was Teddy in with you?" Jess nodded, not trusting her voice, and Dev gave a grunt. "He'd be raising hell if it was a prowler," he said noncommittally.

"I...guess," she whispered. She was going to have to tell him sooner or later. Dev didn't say anything, and the silence seemed to pull tighter around them, filled with that same electrical tension that had been between them, recognized but unacknowledged, all day.

It made her uncomfortably aware of how late it was, of the fact that she was standing there with nothing between her and Dev's hooded gaze but a couple of all-too-thin layers of lace and ribbon. Of how tall and broad-shouldered he seemed to be, filling the room with an aggressive male presence she found distinctly unnerving.

He was naked to the waist and his jeans, obviously pulled on quickly, gaped at the unbuttoned waistband. They rode dangerously low on his narrow hips, revealing much more muscle-corded belly than she was entirely comfortable with, and there was something about the way he was looking at her that made her suddenly remember the raw sexual hunger in his voice that afternoon.

Odd that she'd never considered that part of it. She'd anticipated his anger and hurt, even his hostility, but she'd somehow never thought that he might still feel anything else for her.

Or she for him, she reminded herself even more uneasily. But seeing him again, being here with him all day, had brought back memories and feelings she'd long since put behind her. It was something she hadn't counted on, and she couldn't help wondering what kind of complications it was going to cause.

Dev seemed to sense her sudden unease. He shifted restlessly, then walked across and slid the metal box onto the shelf in the broom closet. "I keep the key under this tin of motor oil," he said suddenly. "Just in case you...need it."

"Taking quite a chance telling me that, aren't you?" Jess replied with forced lightness. "I've got a few grudges of my own, you know."

"If you didn't shoot me during the year and a half we lived together," he said roughly, "I doubt you'll do it now."

He closed the closet door and turned around just as she went to walk by him, and they both stopped awkwardly. He was so close that she could see the faint scar angling across his ribs where he'd fallen on a picket fence when he'd been fourteen, the uglier puckered one on his left shoulder where he'd been shot while trying to bust a drug dealer years later.

It brought back a flood of memories and she swallowed, aware of the clean, masculine scent of his skin, the slow rise and fall of his breathing, the way his chest hair swirled down the muscled contours of his body, narrowing as it traced an evocative line down his abdomen and belly to disappear beneath the gaping waistband of his jeans.

Strange, how she remembered those details while forgetting how tall he was, how solid through the shoulders and chest. She let her eyes trace upward, following ridged muscle and smooth, tanned skin to the V of his collarbone, a little uneven on the right side where he'd broken it playing football in his last year of high school. Higher still to the strong sweep of his jaw and that stubborn McAllister chin, his mouth with its surprisingly lush lower lip...

It was only then that Jess realized he'd been watching her, his eyes narrowed and glittering with an almost predatory intensity. There was something so primitive and hungry in that piercing gaze that she stepped back involuntarily, discovering only then that she was trapped against the counter.

Suddenly flustered, she looked away, desperately trying to think of something to say, somewhere to look other than that expanse of naked, tanned skin. "I...umm...your hand! I should change the bandage."

She reached out to grasp his hand but before she could touch him, Dev's other hand flashed out and caught her by the wrist. His eyes burned into hers and Jess froze as he reached up with his bandaged hand and ran his fingertips lightly down her cheek, then brushed a tangle of wayward hair back from her face, his touch a caress.

"I dream of you, lady," he breathed, his gaze moving slowly over her face, feature by feature.

"Dev..." Almost tentatively, Jess reached up to touch his face, letting her fingers linger on his cheek, his mouth. "I never meant to hurt you, Devlin," she heard herself whisper. "I loved you so much it still hurts to think about it. That's all I ever wanted...just to have you love me back, even a little."

"I wanted to, Jess." It was a harsh sound, torn out of him. "You'll never know how much I wanted to!"

"Oh, Dev..."

She didn't realize he was going to kiss her until his mouth was on hers, and even if she'd wanted to pull away she couldn't have as he cupped her head in both hands, holding her firmly. His mouth plundered hers in a deep, driving kiss that sent her senses into a tailspin and she felt dizzy and disoriented, the taste of him so achingly familiar even after all this time that her body responded before her mind had even fully comprehended what was happening.

Raw desire spilled through her like a tidal wave and she whimpered against his mouth, every nerve ending on fire for the touch of him. He responded with a growl of assent and suddenly he was pressing her against the counter, his half-naked body moving evocatively against hers as his kiss deepened hungrily.

He thrust one blue-jeaned thigh between hers and pressed it against the feminine softness of her, the friction of denim against satin so erotic that Jess groaned. She moved helplessly against him, shuddering as her body betrayed how badly it needed him, and Dev moaned something in return.

Panting, he grasped the thin spaghetti straps of her nightgown in both hands and pulled them down over her shoulders roughly, baring her to the waist, and Jess gave a low cry as he tore his mouth from hers and lowered it, capturing her breast, tongue and teeth caressing the aching nipple until she thought she was going to faint. His hands were on her, large and warm and calloused, the touch of them like magic, and then he slipped them around her bottom and lifted her against him.

He drew his thigh up to open her for him and he fit himself intimately against her, his body so vitally aroused that even through denim the touch of him was so explicit that Jess gave a soft moan. She arched a little to cup him more fully, moving against him, wanting him. She heard his breath catch and he groaned, fingers tightening convulsively around her bottom as he moved his hips urgently and then he was kissing her again fiercely, his tongue wrapping around hers in silken, rhythmic caresses.

She felt more than heard him groan again, a deep sound of torment and agony torn from the very depths of him, and a violent shudder ran through him. He went very still, not even breathing, then he shuddered again and pulled his mouth from hers, panting, his breath hot against her as he lowered his face into the hollow of her shoulder.

She started to slip through his hands and he released her, letting her slide slowly down until her feet touched the floor. She staggered slightly for balance as her knees buckled unexpectedly.

"Lord, Dev..." Trying to catch her breath, Jess rested her forehead against his chest. His skin was hot and moist and she could hear his heart pounding like a freight train, heard him swallow convulsively.

"Damn you..." he whispered with sudden savagery. "Not again . . . not again!"

"Dev, what—?"

But it was too late. He was gone, stumbling away from her as though unable to bear even the touch of her hand.

But not before she'd seen his face. Harlequined by moonlight and shadow, it had been a mask of anguish and desperate pain. And what she could have sworn had been the glitter of tears.

"So, boy—you given any more thought to takin' the job?" Tulley helped himself to another generous helping of pancakes, drenching them with syrup. Picking up his fork, he cut off a huge piece of dripping pancake and maneuvered it into his mouth, chewing with relish as he eyed Dev from across the table. "Place could use someone as knows what's what."

Dev took another drag on the cigarette, then butted it out, eyes narrowed against the smoke as he expelled it in a thin jet. He'd quit smoking nearly two years ago, but this morning he'd found himself digging through drawers and cupboards for the pack he knew was there somewhere, swearing fervently under his breath the entire time. There were some days when it seemed important to withstand temptation, and others when he frankly didn't give a damn. And this was one of them.

Tulley wiped his mouth with the back of a meaty hand and leaned back in the chair with a sigh of satisfaction. It creaked in protest as his considerable weight shifted, and he reached for the coffee cup and downed half the contents in one long swallow, watching Dev speculatively over the rim. "You'd be a shoo-in, boy. People around here like you. More important, they trust you."

Dev managed a grim smile, reaching for his own coffee. "Save your breath, Tulley. I told you three months ago I wasn't going to run for your job when you retire, and I meant it.''

"Folks'd feel safe with you in charge, being a big-city cop yourself an' all."

The knot in Dev's belly tightened and he took a swallow of coffee. "I'm not your man. I'm through with all that."

Tulley's shrewd gaze held his until Dev finally looked away, taking another swallow of coffee. He pushed the empty cup back and eased himself to his feet, wanting another cigarette but refusing to give in to the urge in front of Tulley. Those faded blue eyes might fool an outsider who saw no farther than the beer-gut and sleepy expression, but Dev knew the mind behind them was razor sharp. And he'd been a cop himself long enough to know how much could be given away by a simple nervous gesture.

"Man's gotta put his past behind him," Tulley said mildly. "Can't pull inside himself and shut out the world because of a little hurt. What's passed is done. Maybe it's time you put them demons to rest, son, and started doing what you were born to do—being a cop, and a damned good one.''

"I'm not a cop," Dev replied roughly, reaching for the cigarettes. He shook one out and put it between his lips, squinting as he lit it and drew on it deeply. He tossed the match into the sink, breathing out a stream of smoke. "You're too good yourself not to have checked my jacket, Tulley. I'm listed as a classic case of burnout, and I didn't get any arguments when I handed in my resignation. They figured I was too far gone to be trusted. I figure they were right."

"Bull," Tulley drawled companionably. "You were hurtin', son. Like any decent man would do. Losing people like that—well, I wouldn't trust a man who didn't go a little crazy after something like that. But you've been healin' long enough, seems to me. Much more, and you're just feeling sorry for yourself. Occurs to me you need us, boy, as much as we need you."

In spite of himself, Dev had to give Tulley a dry smile. "Medical Association know you're playing psychologist, Tulley?"

Tulley gave an amiable grunt. "Don't need no shrink to see when a man's in pain, son. You radiate hurt like a stove radiates heat. I'm just *sayin'* you might want to give the job some thought, that's all."

"And I said to forget it."

Tulley shrugged. "Townsfolk don't see it that way. Seen a petition or two goin' around to put you in by acclamation."

"Damn it, Tulley, I'm telling you that I'm not—" Dev stopped short as some movement in the doorway made him look up and he found himself staring into Jess's chocolate-brown eyes. The unexpectedness of it made his stomach pull so tight his breath caught and his mind wheeled, still not used to seeing her there in the familiar contours of his world.

It annoyed him, how easily she managed to catch him off balance like that. Sudden memories of last night spun through his mind—skin like hot silk, the honey-sweet taste of her mouth under his, the tiny indrawn moan when he'd pressed himself so intimately against the feminine softness between her thighs . . .

He wrenched his gaze from hers, turning away and stabbing the half-smoked cigarette into the sink. It sizzled against the wet metal.

"You still smoking those things?" Jess asked mildly, walking into the kitchen as though her presence there was completely normal.

"No." Dev looked around at her sullenly, not knowing where the anger was coming from. Not caring. Welcoming it for the barricade it provided against all the things he didn't want to have to think about just yet.

Her eyes held his for a heartbeat, calm on the surface, but it was only when she looked away that he realized she wasn't quite as serene as she was letting on.

Tulley heaved his bulk to his feet with astonishing grace, whipping his sweat-stained Stetson off and shoving a hand the size of a coal scoop toward Jess. "Name's Tulley, ma'am. Frankie Hudson said something as to there bein' a lady here an' all, but I didn't realize..."

...*that you'd spent the night,* Jess finished for him silently, nearly laughing aloud at the expression on his jowly face. She put her hand out gingerly but his fingers folded around hers with incredible gentleness. "It's nice to meet you—" she glanced down at the police badge pinned to the pocket flap on his khaki tunic "—Chief."

"Jessica Elliott," Dev growled ungraciously, not even looking at her.

"Elliott..." Tulley repeated thoughtfully. His brows pulled together. "That name sure does sound familiar somehow...."

Jess felt herself stiffen instinctively. "My husband was Gary Elliott," she said crisply. "He was on the Seattle police force until he was killed two years ago. You may have heard the name."

He'd heard the name, all right, Jess thought angrily. Gary's name was bad news, and bad news carried fast. She'd seen that same puzzled expression before, the slow dawning of understanding. And then the hint of disgust or morbid curiosity. Or both. She held Tulley's pale blue gaze almost defiantly. Say it, she dared him. Come out and say it: your husband was a bad cop. Your husband dirtied everything law enforcement is all about.

But Tulley simply nodded. "Not easy for a woman, losing her man like that," was all he said, his sympathy too forthright to be anything but sincere. "Takes a special kind of woman to marry a cop. Lucky enough to have one myself, so I know. But that don't make the loss any easier."

Jess's instinctive defensiveness vanished suddenly, and she smiled a trifle wryly. "Thank you. Losing Gary *was* hard, but I've managed to come to terms with it."

"That'll be your daughter outside, more 'n likely."

Jess nodded. "Heather."

Tulley nodded again, even more thoughtfully, his gaze drifting across to where Dev was leaning against the counter, long legs crossed, handsome face closed and inexpressive as he watched them silently.

He knows, Jess thought with amazement. One look at Dev, and he knows. Heather has his eyes and that same strong mouth, that way of looking you straight in the eye . . . she couldn't be anyone's daughter but Dev's.

"I hope you saved me a pancake or two," she said quickly, keeping her voice light. "More coffee, Chief Tulley?"

Those shrewd blue eyes hit hers and held them, and in that instant Jess knew her instincts about this fat old man had been right on the money. He used his easygoing drawl and his beer belly and his benign, jowly face to keep people off balance, but Chief Tulley was as sharp as they came. He'd understood almost intuitively that Dev didn't know yet, and he was gentleman enough to keep the knowledge to himself.

"Thanks, ma'am, but I've gotta go. There was a break-in down at Leila's Bar-And-Grill last night. Kids, prob'ly. They'll be long gone now, but I gotta fill in the forms and make it *look* as though I'm doin' something constructive." He settled his hat over a thatch of wavy gray hair and smiled at her, extending his hand once again. "Nice meetin' you, ma'am. Hope you'll be stayin' a while."

"Thank you," Jess replied noncommittally.

A hint of a smile brushed his mouth. "Good place to relax," he told her, holding her gaze for a moment longer than he needed to. "Safe little place, Whiskey Island. Not too many strangers about this time of year. And them what do come across . . . well, I keep an eye on 'em. If you catch my drift."

Before Jess could reply, he touched his hat in a lazy salute and strode toward the door, hitching his holster and belt up. "Thanks for the breakfast, McAllister. And think on that job some more, hear?'' He shoved open the screen door and walked out into the sunshine, not looking around. ''I'll be in touch.''

Jess turned the heat on under the griddle and stirred the leftover pancake batter, not looking at Dev. ''What was that all about . . . keeping his eye open for strangers, I mean?''

Dev shrugged, moving across to the table and pouring himself more coffee. ''You'll have to ask Tulley.''

Jess gave him a thoughtful sidelong glance, thinking about him prowling the house last night, gun in hand. Maybe she hadn't been as adept at hiding things as she'd thought. She should know better than trying to keep the truth from a man whose business it was to recognize a lie in any of its disguises.

''Frankie mentioned something about a job offer yesterday,'' she said quietly, deciding this wasn't the time to confront him about why she was here. She dropped three puddles of batter onto the hot griddle. ''Are you going to take them up on it?''

''Up on what?'' Dev growled, pacing restlessly.

''Running for office when Tulley retires,'' Jess said with deliberate patience. ''It sounds as though the entire community is behind you.''

''I don't want the job,'' Dev told her with an edge in his voice. ''Damn it to hell, why won't anyone listen to me when I—'' He caught the rest of it and wheeled around to stare out the window, a muscle ticking in his cheek as though he had his teeth gritted. ''I'm out of that kind of business, remember? And the last damned thing I want is a bunch of people depending on me for *anything*.''

There was anger in his voice. Anger, and something else. Pain, perhaps. Anguish. Desperation. It made Jess frown, and she looked at him, a tendril of doubt working its way through her. The community of Whiskey Cove had asked for help and he was rejecting it out of hand. She was here asking for help, too. Would he do the same to her? And what kind of further pain was her asking going to cause?

Damn it, maybe she *had* made a mistake. Maybe this wasn't the time to—

She shook the doubt off roughly, swearing under her breath as she realized the pancakes were burning. Right time or wrong time, she reminded herself grimly, she had no choice. Rich Starkey had taken that away from her.

"Have you eaten, or did Tulley get it all?" she asked over her shoulder. "These are a little overdone on one side, but they're edible."

"I'm finished." He set the mug down on the counter and turned away, still refusing to meet her eyes, and Jess felt a jolt of instinctive anger as he strode by her and out the back door, the screen door slamming emphatically in his wake.

Just as abruptly, she fought it down. God knows, he deserved a bit of sullen anger at finding her still here.

It couldn't be easy for him. She'd had time to deal with a lot of the emotions that seeing each other again brought back. Not long—two days from when she'd made the decision to when she'd actually arrived on his doorstep—but long enough to prepare herself for what was to come.

Dev, on the other hand, hadn't had any warning at all. He'd just crawled up out of a two- or three-day drunk to find her there like the remnant of some dream that wouldn't go away, second of a one-two punch of bad memories that had started when he'd picked up his mail and had opened that envelope from Laurel Conroy's parents.

The door banged open again and Heather came bounding into the kitchen, dark hair flying, cheeks ruddied with salt air. "Hi! You cooking pancakes?"

"You were up pretty early this morning."

Heather shrugged, grabbing a plate from the cupboard and coming over to stand beside Jess. "Teddy wanted out, and you looked like you were going to sleep *forever*." She wrinkled her nose, looking at the three pancakes Jess was sliding onto her plate. "Yuck! Those are burned."

"Well-done. There's a difference. You didn't go too far, did you?"

"Of course not." Heather gave her the arch look of a seven-year-old whose intelligence has just been questioned. "I'm not *that* dumb!"

"Sorry," Jess murmured, hiding her smile as she poured more batter onto the griddle. "How about saving me some of that syrup?"

Heather sighed dramatically and set the bottle down, licking her sticky fingers. "Is Mr. McAllister mad at us?"

"Not specifically." Cradling her coffee mug, Jess leaned against the sink and looked out the window to where Dev was chopping wood with the grim determination of a man with things on his mind. "He's just a little ticked off at everything in general this morning. Don't take it personally."

"He was sure grumpy this morning! He just sort of grunted when I asked him if he wanted some toast."

"A man of little words, our Devlin." Jess took a sip of coffee, eyes narrowed against the steam as she watched Dev attack another block of wood. "He's dealing with a lot right now, that's all. I told you about some of it...about the woman and little girl he was trying to protect who died, and how he quit the police force right afterward."

"And about Daddy," Heather said thoughtfully. "About how Mr. McAllister was there the night that man shot my father."

"That, too," Jess replied quietly. "They'd been best friends once. It's really hard when you lose a best friend...."

As she had, Jess reminded herself. She'd lost not just one, but two. And of all the hurtful things that had happened, losing Dev's friendship had perhaps been the worst.

"Can I go down by the water with Teddy and look for stuff?"

Jess groaned inwardly, knowing that "stuff" could include everything from harmless bits of driftwood to stranded whales. "Only if you don't bring back anything that can walk, swim or fly. And if you promise not to go out of sight of the house."

"Promise. Come on, Teddy!" Heather slid off the chair and grabbed her jacket with one hand and the last pancake with the other, eating it as she ran for the door. Teddy leaped after her, barking and gyrating in excitement.

"If you see anyone out there, I want you to come back here on the double. Anyone at all, okay?"

Heather nodded, her mouth full, already backing out the door. Then she turned and bolted down the steps with Teddy in hot pursuit.

Jess stood at the window for a few minutes longer, watching her daughter race toward the rocky shoreline. Like a young mountain goat, Heather scrambled over drifts of storm-tossed driftwood and logs and wave-smoothed rock, and Jess had to smile.

Then she looked back to where Dev was stacking split wood, and the smile faded. Rich Starkey would figure out where she was sooner or later. And she had no illusions that he'd do whatever he thought necessary to get the information he thought she had.

Frowning, she removed the griddle from the heat, then walked across to the percolator and poured herself a mug of fresh coffee. She poured a second mugful, adding a splash of cream and a generous helping of sugar the way he liked it, and carried them both outside.

He didn't look up when she walked across to the lean-to that sheltered the woodpile, although she knew darned well that he saw her. There was a cool breeze coming in off the water but he'd stripped to the waist and his naked torso gleamed with a light sheen of sweat.

Jess watched him in silence for a moment or two. He swung the ax with powerful, rhythmic strokes, the muscles across his tanned back and shoulders bunching and rippling as he moved, and he attacked each block of wood as though he had a deep personal grudge against it.

The ground was littered with fresh chips and the air was perfumed with the scent of freshly split pine. Dev rested the head of the ax on the ground and leaned down to pick up a cleanly halved piece of wood. He repositioned it, then swung the ax up and around and brought it down in a savage blow, pausing only long enough to toss aside the two halves before reaching for another.

The tall pines around the house murmured as a light wind fingered their upper branches and Jess drew in a deep breath of tart-scented air, feeling it curling down her throat like fine champagne. "It's beautiful out here."

Dev just gave a grunt she was free to interpret as she chose, not bothering to look at her. "You're damned if you're going to make this easy, aren't you," Jess said conversationally. She set his mug on a nearby block of wood, then leaned against the shed and watched him ignore her. "We have to talk."

"About?" Dev swung the ax down and the wood split with a crack. He picked up the two halves and tossed them onto the growing pile beside him. Straightening, he wiped his face with his forearm. His eyes brushed hers, cool as stone.

"About last night, for one thing. We can't just pretend it didn't happen."

"I'd say that about covers it, wouldn't you? It happened. It does now and then. You know that by now—you're a big girl."

"Damn it, Dev, stop shutting me out!" Jess pushed herself away from the lean-to angrily. "God, you drive me crazy when you do that!"

He let the ax rest on the next piece of wood and slipped her a sidelong look. "What is it I'm supposed to say, Jess?" he asked in a low, angry voice. "Just what the hell do you want from me?"

"I want you to talk to me," she told him in exasperation. "That was no sweet, for-old-times'-sake kiss we indulged in last night—we came within a cat's whisker of making love right there on the kitchen counter! The least you can do is talk to me."

Grim-faced, he raised the ax and swung it down in a violent arc and the two pieces of wood went flying. He worked the blade free of the chopping block where he'd embedded it, muscles rippling under the sweat-sheened skin of his back, his jaw set in that way she recognized only too well.

"What is your problem, Devlin?" In spite of her best efforts, a hint of amusement got through. "Afraid I'm going to misinterpret last night as something meaningful and decide to stay?"

He gave her such an odd look that Jess had to laugh. "Last night didn't mean a thing, Dev. It was about yesterday, that's all. Just spontaneous combustion. A man and a woman, a lot of memories, a lot of unfinished business."

"You figure that's what last night was?" He sounded angry. "Unfinished business?"

"What would you call it?"

"A mistake."

"Damn it, Devlin," Jess said with forced calm, "you've got no right to treat me like this. I'm not some nameless woman you picked up in a bar last night and brought home drunk. I won't just conveniently disappear—and neither will what happened between us last night." She turned and started to walk away when he reached out and caught her by the arm, pulling her around to face him.

"Wait, Jess." His eyes held hers, troubled. "Damn it, I didn't mean that."

"Then what did you mean?"

"You're Gary's wife!"

"No, Dev. I'm Gary's widow." Jess's voice snapped through the cool morning air. She stared at him, seeing the anger and frustration in his storm-gray eyes, the pain. "My God," she whispered suddenly. "Is that what this is all about, Dev?"

"No!" He wheeled away and slammed another piece of wood onto the block, lifting the ax again. "Yes," he said more quietly. "Hell, I don't know!" He looked at her again. "I wanted you so bad last night I was half-crazy with it, but..." He frowned. "It just didn't seem right. You married Gary...."

"Gary's been dead for two years," Jess reminded him gently. She ached to reach out and comfort him, knew she didn't dare.

He nodded heavily, then eased his breath out and rested the ax on the block, leaning on it. "It caught me by surprise, Jess, that's all. One minute we were like strangers, afraid to even look at each other, and the next we were going up in flame and I couldn't keep my hands off you."

"It...wasn't exactly what I'd expected, either," she allowed herself to say quietly.

"It *was* good." He gave her a half smile, his eyes warming as they met hers. "Just holding you again. Damned good."

"It was always good with you, Dev," she whispered.

"Yeah."

Their eyes caught. Held. After a breath-caught moment, Jess let her gaze slip from his, feeling her cheeks turning a distinct shade of pink. "And you can still make me blush," she said with a soft laugh. Then she frowned very slightly, rubbing at a smudge of dirt on her hand. "I...umm...don't want you to think that was why I came out here, Dev. It *has* been an awfully long time since...I mean, I didn't intend to—"

"I didn't think you had, Jess," Dev interrupted quietly. "It's been a hell of a long time for me, too, if you want the truth. So let's just put last night down to two normal, healthy people giving in to the moment, and leave it at that, okay?" He gave a sudden snort of laughter. "Hell, we never were any good at withstanding temptation, let's face it. Whatever other problems we had, that was never one of them."

In spite of herself, Jess had to laugh. "Like that afternoon in the tree house on my nineteenth birthday? You'd just graduated from the academy and we decided to pop that bottle of champagne to celebrate. You said we should take it up to the tree house and we...umm..." She shrugged, suddenly embarrassed.

Dev's smile turned rakish. "We got a little beyond the kissing stage *that* afternoon, sweetheart."

"A little," she said with a laugh, her blush deepening.

"You were the one who started it with all that reminiscing about how much fun we'd had up there as kids."

"Seems to me that we'd been fighting temptation for about six months at that point," Jess reminded him mischievously. "Then you popped the cork on that champagne, and one thing sort of led to another."

Dev broke into a broad grin, his eyes capturing hers, warm with remembering, and in that instant Jess felt something shift between them, a release almost, like a breath that's been held for too long.

Dev felt it, too. His gaze held hers for a moment longer, then he shook his head suddenly, chuckling, and set the ax aside. "Talk about spontaneous combustion. It's a wonder we didn't send that poor old tree up in smoke."

"Not that spontaneous," Jess reminded him dryly. "It didn't occur to me until years later that tree houses don't normally come equipped with a convenient little box of contraceptives. When did you put them up there, anyway?"

Dev's grin turned mischievous. "Gary and I used to keep a box stashed up there for years. Just in case."

"Just in case?" Jess echoed indignantly.

He gave an expressive shrug, his eyes warm with teasing. "Gary bought the first box when we were fifteen and he was dating Allison Grimes and hoping to get lucky."

"Gary and Allison Grimes...?" Jess's voice rose and she stared at him in astonishment. "In *my* treehouse?"

"Only in his dreams," Dev assured her with a laugh. "Although I think he got luckier with that little redhead who lived over on Oak Street."

"Roberta Madison." Jess arched an eyebrow. "Every guy in town got lucky with Roberta if the rumors were true." She

Four

Just what he'd been expecting, Dev didn't know. But it sure as hell hadn't been that. He straightened slowly, looking down at her. "What do you mean, kill you?"

She ran her fingers through her wind-tousled hair, looking pale and frightened. "I know it sounds crazy. I thought I was just imagining things at first. But then there was the break-in and the phone calls and the man at the school who tried to get Heather in the car and...and then when Starkey told me he'd hurt Heather if—"

"Starkey?" Dev's eyes narrowed. He swung the ax to the ground and wiped the whetstone on his thigh, slipping it into his hip pocket. "Rich Starkey?"

She nodded, her eyes holding his. "I think he's going to kill me, Dev. And Heather. Even if he finds the money, he's got to get rid of me. I'm the only person who can link him to it."

He had no idea what she was talking about. The only thing that made any sense—the only thing he'd really heard—had been the name: Rich Starkey.

He hadn't heard it in over two years, but it still sent a pulse of dull anger through him. Anger, and a sudden flash of memory: a Seattle wharf late at night, moonlight spilling through the chill air. Gary's eyes drilling into his, defiant and sick with shame at the same time. A gunshot ringing out . . .

"Starkey." He let it linger in his mouth, tasting it. Then, abruptly, he looked at Jess, eyes narrowing. "How does Starkey fit into this? He's still in prison. I put him there, remember?"

"You didn't know. . . ? He's out, Dev. About three months ago. That hotshot lawyer he had got him out on early parole . . . some sort of community service program or something. They made a big deal out of the fact he was a cop—*had* been a cop—and about his service record and everything."

"Out?" Dev stared at her in disbelief. "I spent the better part of a year building a watertight case against the guy!"

"They appealed. Starkey put on this big song and dance about how he'd lived an exemplary life until he started taking drugs because of job stress. He assured the court that he'd reformed and had gone through rehab and all the rest."

She looked up, her eyes filled with anger. "He told them that Gary had been behind it all, Dev. That Gary led Starkey, Brad O'Dare and Randy Burton into a life of crime." Jess gave her head a toss. "Who was going to contradict him? Gary was dead, O'Dare was in jail and would have said anything to get out and Burton was so scared of Starkey you could smell it."

"Exemplary life, my—" Dev swallowed the rest, anger burning at his throat. "Starkey was rotten from the core out. He was running a hundred scams! He was getting a cut of the action from pimps and drug dealers in return for not hassling them, kickbacks from gambling operations and at least two stolen car rings, and he shook down every two-bit hood and creep on the street for what they could afford. I know of at least twice that he destroyed evidence for a price, although I wasn't able to pin it on him.''

Dev lifted the ax and swung it down angrily, sinking the blade solidly into the block. "Damn it, I can't believe they'd just let the guy walk!'' He'd spent a year working hand in glove with Internal Affairs to get enough evidence to put Starkey and the others away. It had been the hardest thing he'd ever done in his life, investigating fellow cops—men he'd worked with, men who put their lives on the line every single day, just like him.

It had become even harder when Gary had become one of the suspects and he'd found himself investigating not just dirty cops, but the man who'd been his best friend since childhood. The man who'd married Jess.

He looked down at her, wondering how much she knew. How much she'd guessed. Did she know that he'd been there when Gary had died? Had maybe, in some macabre way, been responsible?

Raking his sweat-damp hair back with his fingers, he swore in a dull, tired monotone, staring out at the lazy ocean swells piling up on the rocks at the mouth of the bay. The sky looked unsettled, as though trying to make up its mind whether to clear or settle in for a week of rain and fog, and the breeze had turned fitful.

How long was it going to take for the past to let him be? He didn't want anything to do with that life, with the man he'd been back then. That's why he was living out here, minding his own business and wishing the rest of the world would do the same.

He looked around at Jess and found her watching him, quiet and thoughtful. "Maybe you should just start at the top."

Nodding wearily, Jess walked across and sat on the edge of the big unfinished deck he was building out the back of the house. She looked small and vulnerable suddenly, and Dev felt something inside him give a little tug as he strolled across to where she was sitting.

"It sounds so . . . Hollywood," she said with an unsteady laugh. "At first I had the feeling that someone was watching the house. Then I realized I was being followed, and about the same time my phone started making those funny noises again."

She smiled wryly and Dev winced inwardly. He'd been the one to authorize the tap on Gary's phone two years ago.

Jess picked up a twig lying by her feet and twirled it in her fingers. "I had no idea what was going on. I called Mac McDonald down at police headquarters. He was very nice about it, but it was obvious he figured I was panicking over nothing. Besides, the widow of a cop-gone-bad doesn't rate much attention."

Dev breathed an oath, eyes narrowing with anger as he gazed down at Jess. She was right, of course. Gary had betrayed his friends and fellow officers, had brought shame on the brotherhood he'd sworn to support. He'd committed the worst sin of all, and Jess wouldn't have been immune to the fallout of anger and bitterness that would have followed.

And it had been his fault, Dev reminded himself brutally. He'd been in charge of the investigation into police corruption that had all but torn the precinct apart two years ago.

"Three weeks ago, while Heather and I were at a movie, someone broke into my apartment. It had been torn apart—furniture slashed, holes punched in the walls, even the mattresses had been cut up. I called the police and they took one look and said it was kids—vandals." She looked up at him impatiently. "There was an envelope on the kitchen counter with two hundred dollars in it, Dev. I'd sold a ton of junk at a street sale the day before and hadn't gotten to the bank—and it was still there, untouched. No kid would leave that kind of money behind."

"Was anything else taken? TV? Video recorder?"

She shook her head firmly. "Nothing."

"He was looking for something, by the sound of it," Dev muttered, half to himself. His frown deepened and he braced his foot on the raised deck, resting both forearms across his upraised thigh. "What else?"

"Two days later, Rich Starkey turned up at the door." Jess's expression hardened. "I told him to get lost. H-he pushed his way in and asked me where the money was. I told him to get out or I'd call the police. He just laughed and said there wasn't a cop on the force who cared whether I lived or died after what Gary had done."

Dev straightened slowly, the muscles across his shoulders tightening. "Did he hurt you?"

Jess shook her head. "He just kept going on and on about the money—that Gary had double-crossed him and it wasn't where it should have been. He obviously figured I was lying when I told him I didn't know what he was talking about, but before he could do anything my neighbor saw my apartment door open and came in to see if I was all right." She managed a fleeting smile. "Todd is built like a stevedore and Starkey left without a backward look."

"Did you call McDonald?" She didn't say anything, just looked down at the twig she was still holding. Dev frowned. "Jess?"

"I called." Her voice was tight. "He said..." She paused, her face going cold with anger. "Well, you can imagine what he said. 'Birds of a feather' was one of his more polite comments."

Dev's whispered obscenity floated away on the breeze.

"Then, three days ago, Heather's teacher called to tell me a car was hanging around the school and that some man had been seen speaking to Heather." Jess shivered, looking up at him. "I'd told Heather a hundred times not to talk to strange men, but she said she'd seen this man before—that he said he was a friend of Gary's."

Dev's back crawled. "Starkey."

Jess nodded, looking pale. "He called that night and told me that if I didn't want anything to happen to Heather I'd better tell him where the money was. When I told him that I didn't have any idea what he was talking about, he...he started saying awful things. About what he was going to do to Heather and me if I . . ."

She shivered violently, her wide dark eyes looking haunted. "That's when I phoned Mary, and she told me you were out here on Whiskey Island. I threw some things in a suitcase and chartered a boat over." Her gaze held Dev's. "I didn't know where else to go, Dev. You're the only one I trust."

The only one I trust.

Dev subdued a shudder. Gary had trusted him. Laurel Conroy had trusted him. Little Shelley Conroy had trusted him, too.

And they were all dead.

He swung away with an oath, his throat sour. If she'd come to him for protection, she'd picked the wrong man. He'd proved beyond question that he wasn't any good to anyone. He couldn't keep his best friend or even a five-year-old child alive. . . .

"Do you know what money he was talking about?" Jess's soft voice jarred Dev out of his brooding. "You spent a year and a half on the investigation that put Starkey in jail. If there had been any large sum of money involved, you'd have known about it, wouldn't you?"

"Rumors." Dev stared out toward the sea, then gave himself a shake and turned to look down at Jess. "There were rumors going around when we pulled the plug on the investigation that a courier for a major drug buyer was on his way to a meet with five million in cold cash. Word on the street was that he never made it—and that the money disappeared."

"Five million dollars!" Jess's eyes widened with shock.

"It was never confirmed—the buyer was hardly going to complain to the police that one of his couriers was ripped off on his way to buy five million dollars' worth of blow. But I do know that a well-known dealer was found floating in the bay with a bullet in him about a week after the first rumors started. And that if he'd had the money with him, it never turned up."

"Are you telling me that Starkey and Gary were involved?"

"Until now, I was never certain, Jess. But there were rumors that Starkey, O'Dare, Burton and Gary—all working vice, all on the same case—knew about the drug buy and intercepted the courier before he got there."

"So you're saying that Gary *was* involved with Starkey." She said it with a kind of weary despair, as though she'd still been harboring a secret hope that he'd been innocent.

To his surprise, Dev found himself suddenly wishing he could lie to her. There had been a time when he'd thought he'd enjoy rubbing her nose in Gary's fall from grace, but there was none of the satisfaction he'd anticipated.

"Yeah," he said quietly. "He got sucked in deeper and deeper. You know what Gary was like, always looking for the edge, always playing the big shot. Starkey's way promised the kind of money a cop's salary couldn't. Easy money at first glance."

Jess nodded, not looking at him. "Meaning Gary was a killer as well as a crooked cop."

Her voice was a little too well controlled, and Dev frowned. "Gary was no killer," he told her flatly. "He was reckless and stupid and in too much of a hurry, but he wouldn't have killed that dealer in cold blood."

"But Starkey could have." She lifted her gaze to meet his. "Gary brought him over to the house a couple of times. There was something cold about him. Something almost evil. He used to...to touch me. It always seemed accidental, but I knew he was doing it on purpose. And the way he'd look at me—" She shivered. "I always wanted to take a bath afterward. I finally told Gary I never wanted Starkey in the house again."

Dev had to fight down a jolt of raw anger, his fists clenching convulsively. Five minutes, he promised himself darkly. All I want is five minutes with him....

"O'Dare and Burton are both dead," Jess said suddenly.

"Both?" Dev looked at her sharply. "I'd heard O'Dare was killed in prison, but the last I heard of Randy Burton, he was working as a security guard down at the docks."

"He was murdered about three weeks ago—if it hadn't been for the name, I'd never have noticed the little bit about it in the paper. The report said he'd discovered an attempted break-in and was shot and killed." She chewed her lower lip thoughtfully. "Do you think Starkey...?"

"I'd almost count on it," he growled, eyes narrowing. "With Gary dead, there were only the three of them left. Starkey could have had O'Dare killed while they were in prison together, and then gone after Burton after he got paroled. With them dead, he had no witness—and the five million was all his."

"Except he doesn't *have* the five million."

Dev nodded thoughtfully. "Gary was probably in charge of stashing it somewhere safe, only he double-crossed Starkey—or simply wanted some life insurance—and moved it."

"And Starkey got out of prison *thinking* he knew where it was ... and discovered it was gone."

Dev looked at her. "You're his only contact, Jess. You're the only clue he has."

"But I don't know where the money is!"

"Starkey obviously thinks you do. And he wants it, Jess. He wants it bad."

He saw the flicker of fear in her eyes and felt a jolt of responding anger, as familiar as an old friend, felt resentment and bitterness spill through him on its heels. She'd married Gary seeking the secure, stable marriage she so desperately needed, and in the end he'd left her widowed and shamed, raising a seven-year-old daughter alone ... exactly what she'd always dreaded would happen. And now she had a killer on her trail, a man who was willing to murder her and her daughter for five million dollars she didn't even have.

For a split second, he was tempted to draw her into his arms. But he caught himself in time, cursing the weakness within him that still made his hand reach for her, still filled his thoughts with the memory of silken flesh and warm laughter and love in the night.

Neither of them could afford the closeness: he for the pain it promised; she for the false safety she'd think she'd found.

Jess stared at the twig in her hand, feeling cold and empty. Funny how she had to hear it from Dev before she actually believed Gary's guilt. Tears spilled, sudden and hot and completely unexpected, and she got to her feet and turned her back to Dev, wiping at her cheeks.

"Jess . . . ?" Dev's voice neared.

"Damn!" She tried to laugh, but it broke with a sob halfway through. "I'm sorry. I th-thought I was over this long ago . . . !"

His touch was hesitant at first, his hands barely brushing her shoulders as though he half expected her to pull away. Then they settled firmly, comfortingly, and without really thinking about it, Jess turned and stepped blindly into the circle of his arms.

They tightened around her as though she'd never been away, closing out the rest of the world as they always had. And for the first time in weeks she felt the fear slide away, felt protected and safe. Dev had always been able to do that, even in the worst moments of her life, and it was reassuring somehow that at least this part of the magic hadn't been lost.

She rested her cheek on his chest, feeling the solid, slow thump of his heart, the familiar warmth of his skin. As naturally as breathing, she slipped her arms around him, caressing his smooth, sun-warmed back, loving the touch of him even now.

"I need you, Dev," she whispered. "I don't know what to do."

Dev went very still. She could hear him swallow, every muscle in his body seeming to grow taut, and he let his arms drop and stepped away from her, his face an impassive mask as he looked down at her.

"I'm out of that now." He turned away and walked back to the woodpile. "There's nothing I can do. It's a police matter."

"Police?" Jess gave a gasp of astonished laughter. "Gary was on the take, Dev! You know what cops are like when one of their own goes bad—there's not a man on the force who'll lift a hand to protect me, you know that!"

"Not everyone's like McDonald," Dev growled. "I'll make some phone calls, get things moving. And I'll get you and Heather under proper police protection until Starkey can be taken care of."

"And if Starkey isn't working alone?" Jess rubbed her arms as a puff of damp wind wrapped around her. "I heard the rumors, too, Dev. That the corruption went a lot higher than was ever proven. That Gary was killed before he could testify and tell who was *really* involved."

Dev gave her a sharp look. "And that's all it was—rumors. I was on that investigative team myself, remember. There was never anything to indicate it went higher than Starkey and the others."

Which wasn't quite true, Dev reminded himself brutally. There were . . . hints. Tantalizing little trails that led nowhere, clues that proved to be nothing at all. He'd hoped to get Gary to agree to spill his guts that night in return for a lighter sentence. But the night had been filled with evil on that dock, and Gary was dead, any secrets he might have had, dead with him.

Jess was looking out across the restless water, hugging herself as though chilled to the bone, and Dev felt something twist inside him. She looked scared and vulnerable and so alone and lost he ached to wrap his arms around her again and tell her it would be all right, that he'd never let anything hurt her.

But it would be lies. He couldn't help her. Hell, he couldn't even help himself! He still woke up nights soaked

with sweat, his heart pounding like a runaway train, seeing
Laurel and her blue-eyed daughter. Seeing, too, Martin
Conroy's face, eyes glazed with terror in those last mo-
ments of life. Seeing Gary...

He swore, shuddering slightly, and turned away. "I
wouldn't be any good to you, Jess," he said thickly. "I've
lost the edge. I can't keep you safe...."

He walked for hours that day. Up to the top of Spy
Mountain, where bald eagles floated tirelessly on pillars of
air just off the seagirt cliffs. Then down again and out to
Whiskey Cove, from there along the rocky shoreline to the
headland where, it was said, the ghostly crew of a ship-
wrecked rumrunner could be seen on moonless nights.

They'd come down from Canada with bootleg whiskey in
the dead of night and come up hard on the rocks just off the
headland. The January seas had swept them and their illegal cargo to the bottom, and old-timers still talked of finding unbroken bottles of the best Irish whiskey washed ashore
after a storm.

Dev had never found one. Or seen the ghosts, either. But
then, he reminded himself grimly, maybe he was just too
busy fighting off his own.

He dreamed of Laurel Conroy that night, and a blue-eyed
little girl who looked up at him trustingly while dragons
hammered at the door. But then the dream shifted and it
wasn't Laurel there anymore, but Jess. And when he turned
around it wasn't just Shelley gazing up at him, but Heather,
too, both wide-eyed and frightened as something evil crept
through the night.

But he couldn't move, frozen helplessly in that slow-
motion time peculiar to nightmares, unable even to shout a
warning as the shadows neared, and then there were only the
screams...

He awoke with the echoes of his own voice still ringing
through his room and he sat up with an oath, bathed in
sweat and panting for breath, heart pounding. The damp,

clammy sheet was tangled around him and he kicked it free, swearing, and swung his legs over the side of the bed. The breeze coming through the open window was scented of salt and it dried the sweat on his shoulders and back, chilling him. Bracing his elbows on his knees, he wearily rubbed his stubbled face, staring at the rug between his feet.

He stood up after a long while and pulled his jeans and shirt on, knowing he wasn't going to get any more sleep. And half afraid to even try, he reminded himself grimly. At least when he was awake he didn't dream.

Smiling even more grimly, he lifted the pillow to check the revolver lying there. He still didn't know why he'd taken it out of its locked box, but there was no denying that he felt better with it close at hand. Not that he thought for a moment that he'd have to use it. Even if Rich Starkey figured out where Jess was, he'd be smart enough to know what would happen if he came after her.

Dev flexed his shoulders, trying to shrug off the tightness across them. He'd always wondered if it had been Starkey up on that warehouse roof with a high-powered rifle the night Gary was killed. Starkey had spent six months in Vietnam, an eighteen-year-old kid with nothing going for him but a steady hand and a good eye, and they'd taught him the killing trade a little too well for Dev's tastes.

Still, he'd never been able to prove a thing. Starkey's alibi had been watertight, and Gary's murderer had never been caught.

Eyes narrowed, Dev checked the revolver, then tucked it back under the pillow. If Rich Starkey came looking for trouble, he was going to find it. Old habits, like old grudges, die hard.

The house was dark and still as he made his way down the corridor to Heather's room. He opened the door silently, quieting Teddy with a gesture, when the dog opened his eyes to see who'd come in. Padding across to the window, he made sure the security latch was tight, then paused momentarily to glance down at the sleeping child.

She was smiling in her sleep, her face untroubled and serene in the moonlight, and he found himself thinking again how much like Jess she looked. There was nothing of Gary in the dark hair and eyes, and even her finely boned features held nothing of her father's image.

A shaft of rank jealousy shot through Dev before he could catch it and he gazed down at the sleeping girl almost enviously. He'd spent six years tormented by the thought of Jess and Gary together. Imagining them laughing and talking and making love. They'd created their own little world, a world that for the first time had excluded him, and it had eaten him up inside whenever he let himself think about it.

Angrily, he shook himself free of it and turned away, quietly closing the bedroom door behind him. A man could spend a lifetime counting his regrets like a rich man counted gold, or dreaming about tomorrows that wouldn't come. But there wasn't much point to it. Better to keep the past and the future where they belonged, and stick to getting through today.

And if the past suddenly turned up on the doorstep one day like his had?

Dev frowned, easing the door to the other bedroom open and stepping silently inside. Common sense said there was no reason to check on her. If Starkey were within a ten-mile radius, Teddy would be tearing the place apart.

But he found himself drawn almost helplessly into the sweet-scented darkness of her room. The air was perfumed with her and he breathed it in deeply, feeling all the old responses stir slightly at the memories it evoked. She was lying on her side, her hair a dark spill of silk across the pillow, the covers thrown back to her waist, and he could see the slow rise and fall of her breathing. One hand lay outstretched, as though she'd been reaching for something in her sleep. Or *someone,* he caught himself thinking.

Him? Or Gary?

Forcing himself to look away, he walked across and checked the window as he had all the others, not surprised to find that although she'd left it up a few inches, she'd tightened the security catch so it couldn't be opened any wider from the outside. He stood there for a moment or two, staring out across the yard to the rocky seashore beyond, then turned and looked down at Jess again.

He could have sworn that she'd been watching him. But her eyes were still closed, her breathing even and regular, and after a moment he told himself he'd just imagined it. Unable to stop himself, he reached down and brushed a stray wisp of hair from her cheek, letting his fingers linger on her warm skin as long as he dared without waking her.

Damn it, she was so tiny. So soft. Images of last night spun into his mind, of the spontaneous, wild passion that had caught them both unaware, of how she'd felt in his hands, the sweet silk of her body, of how he'd ached to slip deeply into her welcoming warmth, not just wanting but *needing* her....

As he'd needed her for eight long, cold years, he realized in despair. He'd fought it with excuses and hard work and pretty dark-haired women he'd bring home and then send away unloved. But it had been Jess he'd wanted all those years. Only Jess....

She awakened near morning and found him still there. He'd fallen asleep in the big wicker chair by the window, one arm dangling, long legs sprawled out, head tipped to one side at an awkward angle.

Watching her, or watching *over* her?

Both, probably.

She remembered waking in the night to see him standing by the window, staring out into the darkness. She'd almost spoken to him but had caught herself in time, sensing that if she did, he'd leave as silently as he'd come. Instead, she'd closed her eyes and had pretended to still be asleep, not knowing what it was that had brought him to her but familiar enough with the complexities of Devlin McAllister to know he wouldn't want the momentary caring witnessed.

* * *

"Mom, can I go fishing?" Heather hit the kitchen door on the dead run, her face shining with excitement. "Frankie's taking Pud and Chris out in the boat and she says I can come, too, if you say it's okay—it is okay, isn't it, Mom? Please?" She drew the last word out like toffee. "Pul . . . eeze, Mom?"

"Fishing?" Jess turned away from the sink to put the last plate in the cupboard, looking at her daughter with concern. "Oh, Heather—that's not such a good idea."

"She'll be okay, Mrs. Elliott." The screen on the kitchen door banged open again and two boys came stampeding in, one of them tall and slender and towheaded, the other a chubby youngster of eight or nine with freckles and sparkling blue eyes.

The taller of the two looked about twelve, and he grinned at Jess. "I'm Chris Baxter, and this is my brother, Pud— short for Pudgy." He deftly avoided a playful punch from the younger boy. "We're just going out in the bay—Frankie's testing the new engine in her boat and said we could come with her."

"Please, Mom?" Heather's face was a study of hopeful anxiety.

"We're not going far," Chris put in reassuringly.

Jess looked across at Heather, seeing the excitement on her face, the glow that only two days of sea air had put on her cheeks. "Heather, I can't let you go out there, you know that. Honey, I'm sorry. But you know what—"

"Ain't nothing goin' to happen to the girl." The door opened again and Frankie Hudson stomped in, flyaway hair mashed down under a misshapen cap, eyes snapping in her weathered face. "She'll be safer 'n houses out there with me and the boys—you don't have to worry about nothin'!"

"It's all right, Jess." Dev's voice was quiet as he came in behind Frankie, but when his gaze caught hers it said everything the words didn't. "She shouldn't be cooped up here like this."

Jess hesitated, watching the hope blossom in Heather's eyes, the pleading. She finally nodded after a moment, praying she wasn't making a tragic mistake. "All right, then—but wear your life jacket."

Heather's face lit up and she bounced across the room to give Jess a fierce hug.

Chris grinned at her. "We'll take real good care of her, Mrs. Elliott. Promise."

Then the three of them were gone, with Frankie on their heels. The door banged closed, Heather's shouted "Thanks, Mom!" hanging in the air in her wake.

Jess watched the three children gambol excitedly across the yard to pile into Frankie's ancient pickup truck, already starting to regret her decision. If anything happened . . .

"Don't worry about it," Dev said quietly from behind her. "Frankie keeps a Winchester 101 over/under twelve gauge under the seat, and she knows how to use it. Even if Starkey were on the island—and he isn't—he won't get near Heather."

Jess glanced at him curiously. "You told Frankie, didn't you? About Starkey, I mean. And Tulley, too. That's why he was here yesterday."

Dev's eyes held hers for a moment, then he shrugged and turned away, walking casually across to the fridge and opening it. "I might have mentioned something about it. It's a small island—it's easy to keep track of strangers. If Starkey shows up, we'll hear about it."

Jess watched him, not saying anything. Once a cop, always a cop, she reminded herself thoughtfully. Dev would have talked to Tulley and Frankie purely out of instinct, all those old habits too deeply ingrained to ignore. As hard as he tried to deny it, there was still a part of Devlin McAllister that cared. A part that knew what was right.

"Thanks, Dev," she finally said quietly. She walked by him and pushed the screen door open. There was no need to say the rest: that she felt safe here. Protected. They were words he didn't want to hear.

She stood on the back veranda and lifted her face to the sun for a moment, drinking in its warmth. Frankie's old truck was rattling its way up the lane to the road, laughter and young voices lifting through the plume of dust that followed them, and Jess smiled, finding herself relaxing for the first time in months.

Dev came out just then to stand beside her, chewing thoughtfully on a mouthful of apple. "Kind of reminds you of us at that age, doesn't it."

"You, maybe," Jess mused, watching the truck as it disappeared up the road in a haze of dust. "Heather's nothing like I was back then." She watched the dust cloud drift away. "I made sure of that."

An eagle soared above the shoreline in wide, lazy circles, its piercing cry wild and desolate. "I grew up watching my mother throw her life away on a man she couldn't have," she said suddenly. "And somehow I convinced myself that marriage was the solution to life's problems. Marriage meant all the happiness she never had. It meant your children had a real father and a normal life and all the love they needed. It meant security, and it meant forever." She managed a faint smile. "I thought my forever kind of man was the answer to it all."

She was silent for a long while, staring at that distant horizon. "But forever kind of men are scarce, if they exist at all, and I'm making damned sure Heather knows that her happiness is in her *own* hands, not someone else's. I don't want her wasting her life waiting for that impossible knight in shining armor to give her life meaning. It's got to come from inside, and it's got more to do with who you are than who you're with. It took me a long time to figure that out...."

She was aware of Dev's speculative look. There seemed to be a hundred unspoken questions suddenly hanging between them and for a split second Gary's presence was so real that she half expected to look around and see him there, grinning that lazy, devil-may-care grin, the three of them together again as they'd sworn to be.

Then the moment was over. Dev stirred beside her restlessly, as though he, too, had felt the touch of the past, and he tossed the apple core out into the yard. A raucous-voiced crow swooped down out of nowhere and pounced on it and Teddy flung himself toward it with a bark. The crow waited until the last instant before picking the core up in its huge beak, then it leisurely lifted off with a powerful downbeat of its blue-black wings. Teddy leaped frantically after it, jaws snapping on air as the bird sailed just out of reach, seemingly enjoying the game.

"I was planning to leave tomorrow," she said quietly, still not looking at him.

"Not until I call McDonald and get some protection set up," he growled. "You're safer here than in Seattle with Starkey prowling around."

"I didn't mean to turn your life upside down, Dev." She looked at him. "If I'd had anywhere else to go..."

"I know." His voice sounded tight. "Don't worry about it."

"But—"

"I said don't worry about it." He shouldered by her without another word and strode through the door and down the veranda steps.

And Jess, watching him as he walked away from her, shoulders rigid, wondered which was making him angrier: she for being here, or he for not sending her away when he'd had the chance.

She should leave, she told herself bleakly. She'd never been one to stay where she wasn't wanted. And yet, where else could she go? Like it or not, Dev was her only hope. As long as he allowed her to stay, she had no choice.

Five

Letting go wasn't as easy as he'd thought it would be.

Dev frowned, staring at the cold grate in the fireplace.

One phone call, two at the most. He figured McDonald would fight it, but the man owed him a favor or two and in the end, he'd give in. Besides, giving Jess and the girl round-the-clock protection was a small price to pay to get Rich Starkey. Even a straight arrow like McDonald bent a rule or two when the stakes were high enough.

So why hadn't he made the call yet?

Dev swore gently under his breath and lit the ball of paper crumpled on the grate, arranging the kindling so it would catch. She'd been here three days now, and with every passing minute it was getting harder to let her go.

He swore again, loudly enough this time to make Teddy lift his head curiously, ears pricked. He didn't want her here. Didn't want her back in any part of his life again. So why didn't he just make the call and put her on the ferry to the mainland and be done with it?

It was torture, looking up and seeing her at unexpected moments during the day. Their eyes would catch and his heart would give that familiar leap and it would be like it was eight years ago, having her tucked comfortably into the corners of his world where she belonged. But then they'd both remember and look away awkwardly, and the other memories would take over.

The rooms seemed filled with her even when she wasn't there, the subtle scent of her hair and skin perfuming the air. He kept finding her things every time he turned around: a pair of muddy sneakers kicked off inside the back door, a book left lying facedown on the arm of a chair, a clothesline scalloped with impossibly sheer underthings that made him swallow hard every time he looked at it.

It was as disruptive as hell having her underfoot, yet every time he found himself contemplating driving into town to the nearest telephone, something seemed to crop up that needed his attention.

Maybe tomorrow, he told himself, staring into the crackling flames. Maybe he'd call tomorrow....

At first, Jess didn't know what had wakened her. She sat up, frowning, and looked around the bedroom, seeing nothing out of the ordinary. There was a faint tapping at the window but it was just a tree branch dancing in the wind, and she could hear the rustle of leaves, the distant boom of the sea. But nothing else.

Slipping out of bed, she pulled on her light robe, then walked the few steps down the corridor to Heather's room. She'd wanted to move the two beds into one room so Heather would be close by at night, but Heather had put up such a fuss about being forced to share a room that Jess had finally given in and allowed Heather her own room.

Heather was sleeping soundly. Teddy lay curled up on a blanket near the foot of the bed and he looked up inquiringly, beating a tattoo on the hardwood floor with his tail in greeting. Jess gave him a pat on the head, then, after checking the window, left as silently as she'd entered.

She was halfway back to her own room when she heard it again: a low moan, then a soft agonized cry. And, a moment or two later, a husky male voice, murmuring something too low for her to make out the words.

Dev's voice. The anguish and pain in it was so real and so achingly familiar that it went through Jess like a knife blade.

They'd followed him, she found herself thinking as she turned instinctively toward his room. Across eight years and heaven knew how many miles, the nightmares had followed him.

She opened the door to his room and stepped into the moonlit darkness, pausing to get her bearings. She could hear him thrashing around in his sleep, pursued by demons, and followed the sound until she found his bed.

He was sprawled on his back, arms flung out, his naked body gleaming with sweat. The sheets were knotted around his legs and he tried to kick them off, groaning, tossing his head from side to side in denial of whatever he was seeing in the troubled depths of his mind.

He threw his head back suddenly, body arching, and she could see the cords in his throat working as though he were trying to shout something. But it was no more than a tortured moan and he started thrashing around again, his right hand clenching as though around the grip of an imaginary revolver.

"Oh, Devlin," she murmured. "Why won't they leave you alone!" It had been like this eight years ago, waking in the night and finding him pursued by things she only half understood. He'd refused to talk about it when he was awake, and after a while she'd simply stopped asking, settling for holding him in his sleep. But he'd resented even that, hating to have her see him vulnerable. Hating the need for comfort.

"Dev?" She sat on the edge of his bed, keeping well out of range of his fists. "Dev, it's me—Jess. I'm right here, Dev. Everything's all right now...."

He moaned something, his face a mask of agony, tossing his head from side to side. "Dev, let it go. Let it go...." Gently, not wanting to startle him, she reached out to smooth his sweat-soaked hair back from his forehead.

He flinched away from her touch, swearing thickly. "I'll get you," he groaned. "Kill you ... you'll pay...."

"Dev... honey, it's all over now. Just let it go, Dev."

"No! Oh, God... no!" It was a shout of horror and torment and he sat bolt upright, gasping for breath. "No...no, not that!"

"Dev!"

His eyes flicked open and he stared at her, seeing yet not seeing. Then, abruptly, he was awake. Panting for breath, he groaned and covered his face with his hands, scrubbing at his cheeks. "Oh, God, not again. Not again...."

Instinctively, Jess slipped her arms around his shoulders and pulled him against her. "It was a dream, Dev. Just a dream."

She felt him draw in a deep, convulsive breath, his heart hammering against hers. "I let him kill her, Jess," he whispered, his voice almost a sob. "Jessie, I let her die... I promised I'd protect her, and I let her die...."

"It wasn't your fault!" She hugged him tightly against her, eyes closed against a sudden welling of tears.

"He suckered me," he groaned, his arms tightening around her so savagely that Jess had to fight to catch her breath. He rocked his forehead against her shoulder in denial. "Telephone call—the oldest bluff in the book. And I fell for it!"

She could hear him swallow. "When I got back...she was dead. He'd killed her, Jess. I promised nothing would hurt her. I promised ...!"

"Let it go, Dev," Jess whispered, rubbing his shoulders and back. "You did everything you could."

He shuddered violently. "They blamed me, Jessie. Laurel's parents... at the hearing. Said I hadn't done my job. Said I'd let him kill them." He swallowed convulsively again. "I tried to explain. But they wouldn't listen. Called me a murderer. A murderer...."

Jess felt sick and cold, trying not to hate the heartbroken parents who'd done this. They'd lashed out at him in their own pain, seeing Dev as the only solid target for their confusion and anger and grief. And he'd been dealing with this, too, on top of his own guilt, his own self-hatred.

"Hold me, Jessie," he whispered. "Love me...."

She turned her head and found his mouth seeking hers, and in the next instant he was kissing her with the desperation of a man who was all but lost. He cupped her head in his hands, fingers tangling in her thick hair, and he gave a low moan as his mouth plundered hers.

Even half expecting it, Jess was caught off guard, found herself responding to his pain and loneliness and need without even hesitating. His mouth moved hungrily on hers, probing, seeking, demanding everything she had to give, and Jess shivered in his arms, wanting to wrap herself around him and draw him down into the warmth and peace of her body, giving him everything he needed. And more. All he needed, she'd give... even now.

Dev growled something, the desperation in his kiss turning to something else, something more elemental and urgent, and suddenly his hands were on her. He pulled her robe off her shoulders roughly, his mouth never leaving hers, and then her nightgown followed and her breasts were bare to his hands and marauding mouth.

Jess had to bite her lip to keep from crying out at the feel of his warm, work-roughened hands, his touch sending an aching warmth spilling through her. She lay back across the bed and drew him down over her, whispering his name in encouragement as his naked body settled along hers, fitting to her as perfectly as it always had. He caressed her with his body, his hands moving now, stroking her back and hips, his touch as sure as only an old lover's can be.

He knew every silken inch of her and Jess murmured with pleasure, giving an impatient wiggle to settle him more completely against her. He was vibrantly aroused, moving against her, pressing urgently against the barricade of the nightgown still draped around her hips. Jess took him between her thighs, already so achingly ready for him that she could have cried out with sheer frustration as she struggled to tug the gown out of the way.

He was moving against her so explicitly that Jess was sobbing now, well past simple want and into a need so vital and urgent that she was half-wild with it, fighting the restraints of the thin garment that was holding him out. She could feel him there, pressing again and again toward the silken heart of her, each incomplete touch of him more erotic than anything she could have imagined. And after a moment or two she quit fighting it and simply drew her thighs up and apart, closing her eyes with a little whimper of pleasure.

Dev groaned and suddenly went very still, swallowing convulsively. He swore thickly. "Damn it, Jessie! I'm sorry. This isn't right...."

"Dev!" Jess opened her eyes, not believing what he was saying. "You can't stop. Please...Dev, you can't do this!"

"Jess, it's not right," he groaned.

"Yes, it is," Jess whispered against his mouth, her fingers tightening in his thick, tangled hair. "Dev, it's all right. It's what I want, too."

"No, Jess." He said it quietly, lifting himself out of her cradling thighs, still so aroused she distinctly heard him grit his teeth with the effort it cost him. "It isn't right, and you know it. It's too easy this way."

"Damn it, Devlin!" She managed a sob of laughter, nearly crying with frustration. "You never had any problem with an overactive conscience before—this isn't the time!"

"I want you so damn bad I'm not going to be able to walk normally for a week," he growled. "But I don't want you like this, Jess. The other day you said we gave in to a bad case of leftover passion—and you were right. But that's not what I want. And you don't either. We need—"

"Dev, I *know* what I need! And it's—"

"I know what you need, too," he murmured, his eyes burning into hers. "Lie still, Jessie. Trust me...."

"Dev, no...." She tried to twist away from his hand, knowing what he planned, but he held her firmly. "Make love to me, Dev," she pleaded. "I *want* you, can't you understand that?"

"It's not me you want," he whispered, starting to stroke the warm, moist skin of her inner thigh. "It's this...."

She'd intended to fight it, hating him for one fierce instant for turning magic into simple physical need. But in the next instant, at the first knowledgeable touch of his fingers, she knew that he'd been right. That he had recognized their mutual need for everything it had been and everything it wasn't.

Nearly four years of sleeping alone, of dreaming of a man's touch, a man's loving...it all came together into a few wildfire minutes so achingly urgent it almost went beyond pleasure. She forgot to fight him or it, forgot everything but the strong, sure caresses of his hand. Sweetly, gently, he eased her into it and through it, and then he gave her the release she cried out for.

It left her shivering and stunned with shock, panting for breath as the last waves of it finally eased, and as he slipped his arms around her tightly and cradled her against him she turned against his shoulder and started to cry.

It was probably time, Dev thought. She was weeping for everything they'd had and everything they'd lost, for Gary, for eight years of broken dreams. For everything that was still between them—all the unspoken anger, the hurt, the bewilderment. He'd cheated her of this part of it. She'd had to weep in another man's arms for all the pain *he'd* caused, and maybe it was right that he hold her now and comfort her.

The room was getting distinctly chilly and he half sat up, still holding Jess, and found the sheet and blankets he'd all but kicked off the bed. He pulled them up and lay back down with Jess in his arms, wondering how anything could feel as perfect as the right woman—even if it was eight years too late.

She lay there quietly for a long while after the sobbing had stopped, and Dev wondered if she'd fallen asleep. Then she started to pull away, not meeting his eyes. "I... umm...should go."

"You don't have to," he told her gently. She glanced at him through her lashes, and he could tell even through the moonlight that she was blushing. It made him smile. "Not going to get all shy on me now, are you?"

"Don't tease me," she whispered, turning her face away. "I can't believe that I...I *flung* myself at you like that."

"I think it was a mutual fling, sweetheart," he whispered, kissing her ear. "Come on, Jessie, you don't have to be shy with me. It's Dev, remember?"

"I'm so sorry! I shouldn't have let things get so...so far. It should never have happened...."

"Jess," he teased gently, "I've known you longer than just about anybody. Who was it who told you all about the birds and bees when you were in first grade? Who was there for you when you got your first period and were convinced life was over because you'd wanted to stay a tomboy forever? Who rubbed your stomach for you every month when you got cramps?" He kissed the side of her throat. "I gave you your first kiss, took you to your first school dance—and I made love to you for the first time. You can't still be shy with me, Jessie. Not after all this time...."

It made her laugh, as he'd hoped it would, and he felt her relax slightly.

"You're a normal, alive, sexual woman, Jess. Gary died two years ago, and I doubt you've had anyone since—I know you, remember. Sex was never something you took on as a recreational activity. It had to mean something." He brushed a damp tangle of hair from her cheek. "Tonight got pretty intimate, sweetheart. I'd be damned worried about you if you hadn't reacted, to be honest about it." He gave a snort of rueful laughter. "I'd be damned worried if *I* hadn't, come to think of it."

She gave a sputter of laughter and turned in his arms, gazing up at him almost wistfully. "The worst thing about these past eight years was losing you as a friend, Dev," she whispered. "I could always talk to you about things I couldn't talk to Gary about. Or anyone else, for that matter." She touched his cheek, letting her fingers linger there. "I missed you."

Dev felt something pull so tight inside him it made his breath catch and he wondered for a moment if he were still asleep, if this was simply part of the earlier dream. "Not even half as much as I've missed you, lady."

"Do you think . . ." She paused, as though half-afraid to finish it. "Well, that . . . that after this is all over, we could be . . . friends again?" She asked it hesitantly. Hopefully. "Nothing more," she assured him hastily. "But it would be nice, knowing I could call you now and then. Knowing that you'd be there if I needed . . . well, to talk."

"I'd like that, Jessie," he whispered, surprised at how deeply he meant it. "I'd like that a lot."

"Good." She smiled again, then took a deep breath and sat up, modestly covering her breasts as she tugged up the top of her nightgown. Dev helped her, trying to ignore the silk of her skin as he drew the thin straps over her shoulders. Trying, too, not to look at the firm thrust of her breasts against the filmy fabric, the long smooth sweep of thigh and leg against the tangled sheets of his bed.

"You . . . uh . . . could stay," he told her, not entirely certain what he was promising. Knowing only that he hated the thought of spending the rest of the night alone. "I still miss waking up in the morning and having you here beside me."

She smiled, looking up at him through her lashes. "I don't think that would be a good idea, Devlin. I somehow doubt we'd get through the night without . . . umm . . ." Her gesture took in the entire bed. "I know *you,* too, remember."

It made him laugh, long and lazily, and he nodded. "Yeah, you're probably right, Scout. Maybe we shouldn't tempt fate that much. Although . . ." He grinned, running a strand of her hair through his fingers. "It would probably be pretty good, now I'm sober."

"I don't have a doubt in the world," she told him with a soft laugh, and again he could tell she was blushing. "Nothing much *did* happen in that shower the first night, by the way. You were . . . well, you were pretty drunk."

He nodded, his smile fading, and thoughtfully, he drew the strand of hair through his fingers again. "If it counts for anything, Jess, I don't make a habit of that. The last time was after Gary's funeral. It's just too damn easy that way. I watched my old man drink himself into his grave, trying to run away from himself."

"I know, Dev." She lifted her face and kissed him gently on the mouth. "You're a good man, Devlin McAllister. And a strong man. Whatever's out there chasing you . . ." She touched his cheek. "If you ever want to talk about it, I'm here."

"There's nothing to talk about," he replied flatly, his voice more clipped than he'd intended. "I screwed up, a little girl and her mother died, I quit the force—that's all she wrote."

Jess looked at him, her gaze holding his for a long moment. Then she simply nodded and turned to slip off the bed. "Why don't you have a shower while I change these sheets?"

He watched her, part of him aching to reach out and draw her back into his arms again. To pull her back across the rumpled sheets and strip her out of that all-too-seductive nightie and ease himself between her thighs and just lose himself in her. He'd make love to her like he used to, long and hard and deep, not saying a damned thing—just reading everything he needed to know in those dark, bottomless eyes as he sought release for both of them.

He swore under his breath, suddenly angry at nothing whatsoever, and rolled off the bed, striding toward the ensuite bathroom.

Hell, it was too easy *that* way, too. A man could use sex like he used good bourbon, losing himself in a momentary pleasure that would only be regretted come daylight. Jess was here because she'd nowhere else to turn, that was all. It was crazy to let himself think anything else. To *hope* anything else. Hope was like a gag birthday gift—you'd get through all the pretty paper and ribbon and find nothing at all inside. Just more hurt. More emptiness. And he was too damned old to buy into the lies it promised....

Jess watched him pad across the room, naked body lean and muscled and gleaming in the moonlight. The shower came on after a moment and she eased her breath out in a sigh. He was like a rock fortress at times, walled off and barricaded, holding everything inside and everyone out.

Fight it, damn you, she whispered under her breath as she violently stripped the sweat-soaked sheets from his bed. Caring hurts, McAllister. But not caring hurts ever more!

"No sign of your boy yet, McAllister." Chief Tulley leaned against the door frame of the spacious work shed where Dev was repairing a winch motor. Jaws sawing on a wad of chewing gum, he looked the picture of a man with nothing better to do, thumbs hooked comfortably in the wide belt that was valiantly fighting gravity to hold up the sagging pants. "You sure he'll come?"

"He'll come." Dev straightened, stretching the muscles in his back, and tossed a handful of gears into a bucket of oil by his elbow. Sweat trickled down his cheek and he wiped it away with his arm, wishing he had a cigarette and a cold beer. "Odds are, that five million is still stashed wherever Elliott hid it, and Jess is Starkey's only link to it."

"And you're certain she don't know where it's at."

"She's clean," Dev said calmly. Tulley had to ask; he was too good a cop not to. "Gary wouldn't have told her what he was into. He was too smart to put her in that kind of danger."

Although the bastard *had* put her in danger, he found himself thinking angrily. That had always been just like Gary, acting first and worrying about the consequences later. "I'll take care of it," he'd say with that jaunty grin. "Don't worry!"

Except he wasn't around to take care of it this time.

Dev caught the direction his thoughts were taking and clamped down across them, hard. He picked up an oily rag lying on the workbench and started wiping his hands, looking at his visitor. "Don't underestimate what you're up against here, Tulley. Starkey's smart, he's as mean as a snake and he knows his way around. And sat in prison for two years, dreaming about what he was going to do with that money when he got out."

"Files say you're the one that put him there." Tulley shifted the wad of gum to the other side. "I don't figure the man's too happy about that, either. I'd guess he wouldn't mind making you pay a little if he gets the chance."

Dev smiled lazily. "Don't worry about me, Tulley. I can take care of myself. You just keep him away from Jessie."

"A fat old man like me could use some help." Tulley scratched his belly leisurely. "Island can't afford but one full-time deputy, but I carry a couple of badges in the car in case of emergencies. Wouldn't take no time to swear you in, son."

"Forget it," Dev rumbled. "I'm out of it, remember?"

Tulley gave a grunt. "So you say, boy. So you say." He shrugged away from the door frame, still scratching his ample khaki-clad stomach. "If you change your mind, you know where I'm at. Until then, I'll keep an eye out for your boy Starkey and let you know what turns up." He turned away, then looked around. "You got a gun, boy?"

Dev tossed the oily rag down. "What do you think?"

"I think you'd better keep it handy, is what I think," Tulley said quietly, joviality gone. "I'll do what I can for you, son, but I'm one old man and this island is a big piece of real estate. Boats come in all the time where I don't see 'em. Folks are keeping watch, but he could be here a week without me hearing about it. You just keep your eyes open."

Dev felt the familiar tightness settle in his stomach and swallowed, trying to shake it off. He had a flash of memory of wide blue eyes, child's eyes, then it was gone. "I'll call McDonald this afternoon," he said evenly. "Arrange proper police protection for her and the girl while they wait for Starkey to make a move."

Tulley just looked at him for a long, thoughtful moment. "Seems to me," he said slowly, "that she'd be a damn sight safer here. Starkey still may have friends on the force...."

"She'll be safer in protective custody," Dev said flatly, turning back to the workbench. He didn't want to talk about it. Not with Tulley. Not with those pale blue eyes looking right through him.

Tulley gave another grunt, then walked back to the dusty police cruiser parked in front of the house. Dev heard it pull out and head back up the road to the highway, but didn't bother turning to look. He was gazing out across the weathered rock shoreline instead, eyes narrowed against the glare of the afternoon sun, the knot in his gut pulling even tighter until he finally saw her.

She was walking along the edge of the water, hands in the pockets of her light cotton slacks, face turned to the sun, looking as casual and relaxed as any summer tourist. She'd been out there for nearly an hour now, and he found himself glancing up every few minutes just to check on her.

Not that she was really in any danger. He had more faith in Tulley than that. But part of him—the ex-cop part—

wanted her nearer to the house where he could watch her more easily.

And another part of him, a part he was just starting to admit to, just wanted her nearer, period.

Which wasn't the way it was supposed to be.

Six

The hillside between Dev's house and the rocky shoreline was a gentle slope, covered with lush grass and wildflowers and a handful of tall, broad-limbed trees.

Perfect trees for climbing, Jess mused drowsily. Or to hold a tree house. In fact, the one she was sitting under would hold a veritable mansion of a tree house. Stretched out comfortably on her back, ankles crossed, her arms under her head, she gazed up at the big tree spreading its canopy across the sky above her.

Where the whim came from, she had no idea—but in the next instant she was on her feet, and in the instant after that she was pulling herself up onto the first low-hanging branch. Laughing with exhilaration, she got her feet under her and stood up, eyeing the network of branches above her for the best way up. How long had it been since she'd last shinnied up a tree—ten years? Twelve?

Ten, to be exact. She smiled with the memory, setting foot on the next branch cautiously and reaching for a solid handhold, then pulling herself up. She and Dev had taken that bottle of champagne up to the old tree house, planning to toast his career. But one thing had sort of led to another, and before the afternoon was out they'd more or less forgotten the champagne in the delights they'd found in each other.

The tree was easy to climb, the limbs well spaced and solid, and it took a scant minute or two to reach the comfortable perch she'd spied from the ground. Two thick limbs branched out from the huge trunk almost side by side, one a little higher than the other to form an almost perfect chair. Straddling the lower of the two, she leaned her elbows on the other and cupped her chin in her hands to gaze happily across the meadow.

She saw Teddy first. He was bounding through the grass like a pup, tail windmilling as he crisscrossed the hillside on his way down. Dev was following, walking down with that long-legged, relaxed stride that had always been his trademark, shoulders back, sun-bleached hair glowing in the sun.

He paused once or twice in his descent and stood scanning the beach, hand shading his eyes, and Jess suddenly realized he was looking for her. She sat up, intending to call to him, then decided to save her breath until he was closer.

It only took him a couple of minutes to reach her tree. She grinned to herself as she looked down at the top of his tousled head. He stopped there, hands on hips, and swore with more feeling than originality as he scanned the hillside and rocky shoreline again. Biting her lip to keep from laughing out loud, Jess leaned over and dropped a handful of leaves and twigs squarely onto the top of his head.

He leaped back with another oath, brushing furiously at himself, and glared up into the offending tree. Then, slowly his mouth lifted in a broad smile. "What in the *hell*," he asked lazily, "are you doing up there?"

"Checking out tree house sites—this is a perfect one." Her gesture took in the entire tree.

"Heather took off with Chris and Pud a few minutes ago. She said she'd cleared it with you first."

"Sort of," Jess admitted doubtfully. "There was something about a spaniel with a new litter of pups and an eagle's nest. She said Chris's father was going to be with them...."

"She'll be fine," Dev assured her. "If Starkey turns up, he'll head straight here. Chances of him stumbling on Heather anywhere else are slim to none."

Jess nodded. "Was that Tulley's car I saw a few minutes ago?"

"In person."

"He's serious about wanting you to run for chief of police when he retires, isn't he?"

"He thinks he is."

"All you talked about when you were a kid was being a cop," Jess said gently, knowing she was treading on very thin ice. "I can't imagine you doing anything else."

"That was a long time ago." He was staring at the water as though there were something along the empty horizon that fascinated him. "A lot of cops burn out. It's one of the hazards of the job."

"And you're happy out here, playing jack-of-all-trades."

"It's a living."

There was something in his voice that made Jess decide not to pursue it further. "Care to come up here and have a look, or are you too old and uptight for that kind of thing?"

He looked up at her sharply, as though suspecting some sort of trick. Then, after a moment, he relaxed and gave a quiet laugh. "I'll show you old and uptight!" he growled, kicking his boots off. His socks were the next to go, then he made a big production of spitting on his hands and eyeing the branch above his head before swinging himself up easily.

The broad branch Jess was sitting on shuddered as Dev swung his full weight up onto it, and he settled beside her with a grin and reached out to ruffle her hair with his hand. "Not so bad for an old man, huh?"

"Not so bad," Jess agreed with a grin.

Those rich chocolate-brown eyes were filled with teasing and good memories, and Dev felt his stomach tighten slightly. Damn it, she was still the most beautiful thing he'd ever seen, with that heart-shaped face and those huge long-lashed eyes that could see right through a man.

He could remember as clearly as yesterday the first time he'd seen her, a gamin girl of seven, all knobby knees and gangly legs, those big eyes peering at him from behind a tangle of uncombed hair.

He'd probably fallen in love with her on the spot, he found himself thinking, although it had taken years for him to realize it. At the time she'd just been another little girl that he'd taken under his wing without thinking about it, so used to the role of protective big brother to his own sisters that another one didn't make much difference.

But then she'd grown up, and things had changed.

He glanced at her, marveling, as always, at how tiny she was next to him. How perfectly female. It was that quality that had hit him like a lightning bolt that afternoon about fourteen years ago. He'd come home from college to discover that the little ragamuffin tomboy with the scabby knees and pigtails that he'd left in the fall had blossomed, seemingly overnight, into a young woman so heart-stoppingly beautiful he could still recall standing there staring at her in disbelief.

She'd smiled at him, blushing like the schoolgirl she still was, and he'd known in that instant that things would never be the same between them. They weren't just best friends from that point on, but man and woman—with all the chemistry that went with it.

It had taken four years for him to do anything about that chemistry, but when they'd finally come together in that tree house on her nineteenth birthday, they'd ignited enough sparks to light up the countryside. It took no effort at all to remember that afternoon, at seeing her naked for the first time, of watching the faint apprehension in her eyes turn to surprise, then to frank pleasure as he'd eased himself into the heated silk of her for the first time and she'd held him in the most intimate embrace a woman can offer a man, trusting him not just with her heart but with the sanctity of her very body.

And in that moment as he'd lain between her thighs, cradling her head in his hands and gazing down into the love-filled depths of her eyes, he'd felt something change within him, a release, almost, as though something tight around his heart had fallen free.

Jess smiled suddenly and looked at him, resting her elbow on a convenient bough and cupping her cheek in one palm, her eyes wonderfully soft as they met his. "Like old times, isn't it?"

The breeze smelled of green grass and the sea, and the branches around them were filled with the sound of rustling leaves and birdsong. "Almost." He looked at her, letting his gaze run slowly over her small, perfect features. Remembering. "It's been a long time, Jessie."

Her eyes held his, sweet and rich and deep enough to drown in. "Too long," she said very softly. "Dev, I..." She frowned slightly and bit her lip, looking away. "I missed you."

He got the feeling it wasn't what she'd started to say, but he didn't care, he liked hearing what she *had* said. He'd promised himself he wasn't going to delude himself into thinking they could ever have any kind of a relationship again, but it wouldn't hurt if they were at least friends. He could risk that much.

"I should have called you," he said suddenly. "After the...funeral. But I just..." He shrugged, reaching out and taking a stray leaf from her hair and twirling it by the stem.

"I never have had a chance to thank you for the flowers and the card." She looked at him. "I'd hoped you'd be at the funeral. It would have made things ... easier."

Dev winced a little, not looking at her. "I was there, Jess. But I stayed back. I—" He frowned, looking away. The memories of those days right after Gary's death were still unclear, filled only with helpless rage and grief. And guilt. "I didn't think you'd want me there," he said quietly. "I didn't want to intrude. So I stood back by the road, under the trees."

"Intrude?" Her voice was soft with disbelief. "Dev, how could you think that? He was your friend, too. You had a right to be there. To say goodbye." She put her hand on his, sighing. "It was hard that day. It was as though no one even wanted to admit he'd been a policeman. No one from the precinct attended, and what few friends did come snuck around as though afraid someone might see them paying their respects to a dirty cop."

Dev squeezed her fingers gently, remembering his own anger that day. It had been gray and overcast, and the group gathered at the graveside ceremony had been embarrassingly small. The department's refusal to acknowledge one of their own—even one who had gone wrong—had been unnecessarily cruel.

"At first I thought you were just like the rest—that because Gary had turned, you didn't want anything to do with him. I was furious with you for weeks—I must have written six dozen letters telling you in no uncertain terms of what I thought of you." She smiled ruefully. "None of which I mailed, thank heaven. I said some pretty horrible things."

"You were entitled," he replied quietly. "The department treated you shabbily, Jess. Gary had gone bad, but that was no reason to abandon his family when they needed support the most."

"Well, I can see their point, too." She stared at their linked hands thoughtfully, smoothing the sun-bleached hair along his wrist and forearm. "I guess this is as good a time as any to thank you for everything you did then, too. With Gary's pension and life insurance and everything."

"Pension?" Dev echoed carefully.

Jess smiled. "You don't have to play innocent, Sir Lancelot. McDonald told me all about it—how you put your job on the line for Heather and me, threatening to quit on the spot if the department didn't reinstate Gary's pension and insurance."

Dev shrugged carelessly. "Shucks, t'warn't nothing, ma'am."

"It was," Jess said with quiet firmness. "You know what Gary was like, spending money like it was water. There was about a hundred dollars in the bank the night he was killed. If it hadn't been for his insurance money and the pension, Heather and I would have been in serious trouble, Dev. Gary's parents weren't in any position to help, and my mother—well, you know Mom and money. She's always one step ahead of the collection agency."

"I figured it was the least I could do, considering—" He bit it off, teeth gritted.

"Considering...?" Jess looked at him curiously.

"Considering we'd all been best friends once," he lied, not looking at her. *Considering I may have murdered your husband,* he added silently. *Considering that if it hadn't been for me you'd still be married right now, and Heather would have a father and—*

He cut the rest of the thoughts off brutally. It was pointless, castigating himself for what *might* have been if he hadn't arranged to meet Gary on that particular dock that night. If he'd listened to his gut instincts and checked the perimeter more thoroughly. If he'd brought backup. If... if... hell, there were a hundred *ifs*....

"I think that in a way he was glad when it finally all came out," she said suddenly, looking out across the wind-rippled sea of grass beneath them again. "He was torn up about it, Dev. I didn't know back then what he was involved in, but I knew something was eating him up. I kept trying to get him to talk about it, but he wouldn't."

She gave him a thoughtful look. "And as strange as it sounds, I think he was glad it was you on that investigating team." Dev gave a snort of harsh laughter, but Jess just continued to look at him with those wide dark eyes, her expression serious. "I mean it, Dev. He was ashamed, he was hurt... but it made it easier, knowing it was you."

"I wasn't easy on him," he grated, not daring to look at her. He'd gone after Gary like a wolf after a rabbit, wanting blood. It had been revenge, pure and simple, and it nearly made him sick now to think of the hate that had twisted his mind during those days. Jealousy and rage had turned what had started as a police investigation into a personal crusade to destroy the man who had married Jess.

"But you were fair," she said softly. "He trusted you to be that, anyway."

"Fair?" He managed a bitter laugh, meeting her eyes squarely. "Jess, I was ready to do anything—*anything*—to get Gary convicted on those charges of corruption. I wanted him brought down, do you understand me?"

She looked at him in confusion. "But... why?"

"You know why," he said more quietly, his eyes holding hers. "Damn it, Jessie—you know why."

Her face crumpled suddenly, and for half an instant Dev thought she was going to cry. He braced himself, but she struggled with the tears for a moment or two, silent, face turned away. Then she drew in a deep, unsteady breath. "I... see," she whispered, head still tucked down so he couldn't see her face. "I didn't realize... after all that time..."

"All that time?" he asked with a rough laugh. "Eight years without you was a lifetime, lady. Six years of knowing he was in your bed where I should have been, making love to you when you should have been mine."

She turned her head slowly to look at him, eyes filled with confusion, and he swallowed the rest of the tirade, the anger vanishing so unexpectedly that he felt nothing but a vast, gaping emptiness. "Hell," he sighed, scrubbing his hand through his hair in weary despair. "I'm sorry. I shouldn't have said that."

"We were separated, Dev. Two years before he was killed."

Dev blinked. Looked at her. "What do you mean?"

Jess smiled gently. "We were going to start divorce proceedings the week he died. It was ironic, in a way...."

Dev swallowed very carefully. "I don't understand. How could you have been separated? I mean, no one knew...." *I didn't know,* was what he meant. *And I would have known.*

"We didn't think it was anyone else's business. And Gary was embarrassed—he didn't like failing at things, and a divorce is a pretty public way of announcing failure. And it wasn't as though I was trying to hurt him or anything. We just ... I couldn't live with him."

"But you were together," he said stubbornly. "At Chief Donaldson's retirement banquet. At—"

"I'd go with him for appearance's sake. When it was over, I'd go my way and he'd go his." She frowned, looking down and toying with a leaf. "He started drinking, Dev. And then there were the drugs—anything new and dangerous, Gary would bring it home. Just for the kick, he used to say. He *didn't* need it." She smiled wearily. "That's what they all say, isn't it. Trouble is, Gary really believed it."

"I knew he was always looking for the edge," Dev muttered. "Always seeing just how far he could go without messing up bad. But I didn't realize...." He gave his head a shake, knowing he shouldn't have been surprised at all. He tried to dredge up the pleasure he knew he should be feeling, the grim satisfaction, but the only emotion he was aware of was sadness.

"He liked the danger and the risk," Jess said. "You know what he was like. Even when we were kids he was always the one getting into the most trouble because he never knew when to quit. I can still remember the day the two of you decided to climb the water tower and Gary had to go that extra distance to touch the lightning rod right up at the peak."

Dev managed a grim smile. "And the day he got the casts off his legs, he was doing handstands on the pillion seat of his brother's motorcycle at sixty miles an hour on the freeway."

"He worshiped you," she said softly. "You were always his hero, Dev. I think, in some weird way, that's what made him so driven. You always seemed to succeed at everything you tried and made it look effortless into the bargain, but it was harder for Gary. So he overcompensated by being the biggest and baddest in everything he took on." She smiled very faintly. "He even died dramatically. Somehow, I think it probably pleased him that he managed to go out while upstaging you."

"Lord, Jess . . ." Dev whispered hoarsely.

"Sorry." But she smiled again, not looking particularly contrite. "I didn't mean to sound flippant, but you knew Gary as well as I did—and you know I'm right. He'd never have been happy dying gently in his sleep at ninety-five, surrounded by great-grandchildren and his grieving widow. He wanted to go out of this world at Mach 10, making as big an impression and causing as much ruckus and noise as possible."

Dev thought of that night. Of the expression of near-defiance in Gary's eyes. The reckless grin that had brushed his mouth just at the end, as though he were having the last laugh on the world after all.

He drew in a deep breath, then eased it out between his teeth and looked at Jess. "For what it's worth, I'm sorry. I know what marriage and all the rest of it meant to you." He smiled ruefully. "Hell, that's what had sent me running in the first place, wasn't it?" Then he let the smile fade and reached out to touch her cheek. "But I'm damned sorry it didn't work out for you, Jessie. You deserved better."

I deserved you, Jessie almost said, deciding in the nick of time that it was still a little too soon for that. She nodded instead, and turned her face to kiss his palm. "It wasn't easy giving up the dream at first. But I finally realized that if I didn't leave, I was just repeating all the mistakes my mother made. She was obsessed with being in love, even if it was with the wrong man, and I was obsessed with being married.''

She smiled again. "When I finally figured all that out, I knew I had no choice. And I had a responsibility to Heather. Gary was a good father when he was around, but that wasn't much of the time. And I didn't like the people he was bringing into our home, the liquor and drugs, the parties.''

She knew Dev was looking at her thoughtfully, and managed a careless smile she knew he saw right through. "When I was a kid, I thought that having a father was the most important thing in the world. But it isn't. Having love and caring and hugs when you need them—that's what's important.''

"So you walked out.''

She nodded. "It was hard at first. I had no money, no real skills...three years of art history doesn't exactly prepare you for the real world. Then I ran into one of my college profs in a coffee shop, and he told me he needed someone to proof and edit a couple of papers he was submitting. By the time I finished that project, three others were waiting to hire me...and I realized I'd stumbled into a good thing.''

"And that's what you're doing now?'' He gave his head a rueful shake. "You've been here what—four days—and I don't even know what you do for a living.''

"I'll have you know, sir, that you're talking to the president, vice president, owner, manager and half the staff of *PrintWrite Editing Services*.'' Jess grinned. "It's desktop publishing, actually, and I handle everything from doctoral papers to baby-care pamphlets from my local pediatrician. I was hoping to just make a living at it, but it's grown so fast I had to hire a full-time assistant last June, and I'll soon be needing another.''

Dev's mouth tipped up in a smile. "Well, I'll be damned. An entrepreneur.''

Jess grinned happily. "It was the perfect job when Heather was small because I could work at home and keep an eye on her, but now I just plain love it." She looked at him for a long moment, then decided to throw caution to the wind. "A person should love what he's doing, Dev. Anything else is just putting in time."

His eyes narrowed fractionally. "Meaning?"

"Meaning you're a cop, Devlin," she replied softly, "not a part-time carpenter and full-time recluse."

"Don't push it, Jess." He swung one long denimed leg over the branch they were sitting on and started back down the tree.

Jess reached out and caught his arm, leaning toward him urgently. "Damn it, Dev, stop running from it! Don't you think I know—"

"You don't know a thing," he said in a low, vibrant voice, wrenching his arm out of her grip. "Not a damned thing!"

"Dev—!"

But he was gone. A moment later he was on the ground, picking up his discarded socks and work boots, and a moment after that he was striding back up the hillside toward the house, his broad tanned back as rigid as stone.

Jess watched him, her heart aching for the pain she'd seen in his eyes for that heartbeat when they'd held hers. Why in God's name had she blurted it out like that, she asked herself furiously, reaching for the nearest branch to swing herself down. A man like Devlin McAllister didn't turn his back on himself and the rest of the world unless the hurt went bone-deep—it would take a surgeon's skill to exorcise it. And she'd blundered in with all the delicacy of a chain saw!

He wasn't in the house when she got there. It was still and silent and cool, and she wandered restlessly from room to room. She turned the radio on and tried to listen to it, but it picked up just two stations and she was too distracted to make sense out of the talk show that was on one of them, and in no mood for the country-and-western ballads of broken hearts and scattered dreams on the other.

Heather came home a couple of hours later. She was sunburned and utterly happy, clutching a fistful of eagle feathers and so filled with details of her day that for an hour or two Jess was almost able to forget Dev. Heather made it through supper without falling asleep, but she was in bed by seven that evening, and Jess was alone again.

Dev still hadn't come in. His old pickup was outside so she knew he hadn't gone far, and it made her heart ache, thinking of him out there alone and hurting. For some reason, it made her think of those times when they'd been kids and she'd go out to the big tree house at night and find him there. He'd be asleep, huddled under the old blanket he kept up there, not daring to go home to the drunken father who saw Dev's protectiveness toward his sisters as a sign of weakness.

Jess frowned, staring down into her cup of cold coffee. She was still sitting at the kitchen table, the only sound that of Teddy's gentle snoring at her feet and the tap-tap of moths banging on the window trying to get to the light. Was that when Dev started to equate caring with being hurt?

Funny, how she'd never seen that connection before. All she remembered of those days was the sheer joy she herself felt in Dev's companionship. He'd been the nearest thing to family she'd ever known, her mother too caught up in her own unhappiness and loneliness to do much else but cry and wait by the telephone for her married lover to call.

And on those nights when Dev stayed in the tree house, she often stayed up there with him. She'd nestle up against him and they'd talk long into the night, dreaming their child dreams, promising always to be there for each other. In those simpler days he talked of nothing but being a cop, and she wove fantasies around the normal respectable family she'd have around her when she grew up, with a husband and kids and more love than you could imagine.

Jess swore under her breath and got to her feet abruptly, tossing the cold dregs of the coffee into the sink. She was too young to be getting maudlin over the good old days! Teddy thumped his tail on the floor and gave her a doggy smile from under the table, and in spite of her less-than-perfect mood, she had to laugh.

"One biscuit, then you're out of here, mister," she told him. She opened the cupboard under the sink where Dev kept Teddy's treats and the dog was on his feet in an instant, poised expectantly. Jess laughed again and knelt to rub his neck and ears as he crunched the bone-shaped biscuit enthusiastically. "You probably think coming out here was the best idea he ever had, don't you?" she asked him. "Beats living in an apartment in the city, hey?"

He gyrated happily, wagging his tail so hard his entire rear end went with it, and she laughed again and wrestled with him for a minute or two before ushering him out the back door for his nightly run. "If you find him out there," she whispered as the dog vanished into the darkness, "bring him home. There are people here who miss him...."

Which was, she decided as she made her way to her bedroom, only a slight understatement. There hadn't been a day in the past eight years that she hadn't missed him. And there probably wouldn't be one in the next fifty or so when she didn't feel the same. Love was, as Heather would disgustedly put it, the pits.

She didn't hear him come in, didn't even know he was there until she came out of the bathroom, still damp from her shower, and looked down the long corridor toward the living room. He had lit a fire and was sitting on the big hassock, forearms on his thighs, hands dangling between his knees, staring into the flames. A man alone.

Jess stood there for an indecisive moment, wanting to go out to him yet fairly certain he wouldn't appreciate the gesture. And besides, she'd been on her way to bed and wasn't dressed for a heart-to-heart. She looked down at the silk nightgown, wondering, not for the first time since she'd gotten here, if it had wound up in her suitcase because she'd been packing in blind panic, grabbing anything that was handy, or if in some deep ever-hopeful recess of her mind she'd thought she might need it.

Finally she opened the bedroom door and tossed her quilted toiletries case onto the bed, then walked down to the living room. Dev didn't look up as she passed behind him, heading for the kitchen. Had he even seen her, she wondered, or was he lost in whatever he was seeing in those flickering flames? Only Teddy, curled up by Dev's feet, glanced up curiously. Then he put his head down on his paws and closed his eyes again.

She made the coffee dark and strong, the way he liked it, then added a healthy shot of brandy as an afterthought and carried it back into the living room. As before, he didn't look up, didn't make any sign whatsoever he even knew she was there.

"There's brandy in this," she said quietly, holding the mug in front of him. "It might help you sleep."

She thought for a moment that he wasn't going to take it. Then he put his hand out and took it from her. "Thanks." His voice was gruff, almost embarrassed, and he didn't look at her.

"Are you hungry?" she dared. "I saved some supper for you."

He just shook his head, not saying anything, and took a swallow of the steaming coffee.

Jess stood there for another moment or two, feeling suddenly awkward, then she just nodded and turned to leave.

Dev's free hand flashed out and caught her gently by the wrist. "Don't go." It was just a rasp of sound, torn out of him, and he kept his face averted, as though hating the weakness that made him ask even that much.

Jess gazed down at him, then very tentatively reached out to stroke his hair. He flinched slightly at the touch but made no effort to turn away, and after a moment Jess knelt in front of him. Gently, she took the mug from between his hands and set it on the floor, then she smoothed his wind-

tangled hair back from his forehead with her hands and
drew his face toward hers, lifting her mouth.

His lips stayed cool and unresponsive for a heartbeat of
time, then she felt them soften under hers, parting willingly
to the delicate touch of her tongue. He made no attempt to
touch her but she could feel his breathing deepen slightly as
she ran the tip of her tongue along his lower lip, then sucked
on it gently, nipped the corners of his mouth.

His tangled hair was sticky with salt air and she ran her
fingers up into it, kissing him less gently, feeling him starting to respond. His mouth moved on hers, taking now, his
tongue meeting hers, teasing it, drawing it into his mouth
where he captured it with consummate skill. Jess sighed with
pleasure and turned her head to put her mouth more fully
under his, feeling the tension in him change, testing his desire as though it were her own.

And then, suddenly, his arms were around her and his
mouth settled over hers, hard and demanding and forceful.
He cupped her head in both hands and kissed her with the
unapologetic hunger of a man claiming what by rights is his,
the silken thrust of his tongue leaving no doubt as to what
he wanted, the pressure of his lips leaving her no room to
argue.

His tongue moved against hers urgently and Jess shivered, feeling tendrils of familiar fire wind their way through
her. It had been like this that first time, too, her body so at-
tuned to the taste and scent and feel of him that even after
eight long years it responded almost instantly to the promise they held. She felt drugged and warm and sleepy, and
sighed again in pleasure as his palm brushed her breast, the
nipple erect and taut and aching for his touch.

He growled something against her mouth and suddenly he
was kneeling, too, shoving the hassock out of the way impatiently, and then he eased her back across the faded rag
rug in front of the hearth. His mouth was still moving on
hers but now his hand was too, stroking her breasts and
stomach, caressing the flare of her hip.

Even through silk, the touch of her was magic. Dev didn't consciously remember when he'd stopped fighting it, knew only that he'd been waiting for this moment all day, knowing it had to happen, that he wanted it to happen. He'd been filled with the taste and feel of her all day, remembering every erotic moment from the previous night when he'd held her, touched her, caressed her, had set her on fire and had watched her burn with it.

It was too late for second thoughts, he realized dimly. Too late for good intentions. All he wanted was to feel her naked against him, to hear her whisper his name, her voice filled with breathless little catches as he touched her, easing his fingers into that secret melting place and knowing he was pleasing her.

And he wanted to capture that one moment in suspended time, that instant when he sank full-length into her and listened to her soft cry, wanted to feel the strong flex of her hips as she wriggled impatiently against him, wanting more, wanting it all. And giving it to her....

He pulled back slightly so he could look down at her. Her eyes were heavy, almost sultry beneath the thick lashes, and her mouth looked lush and swollen, still moist from his. He didn't say anything, knowing she could read everything he wanted in his eyes.

"Not here," was all she whispered. "I don't want Heather to come out and find us...."

It was that easy, he realized with faint wonder as he picked her up in his arms and got to his feet. No questions, no hesitancy, no doubts. Just the two of them, the way it had always been. The way it was supposed to be.

His bedroom was dark and cool, and Dev kicked the door closed behind him, his mouth already seeking hers as he fumbled behind him with one hand to lock it. Jess started to slip out of his arms and she gave a breathless laugh, reaching up to catch a fistful of his hair in each hand and pull his mouth firmly down to hers again, welcoming the urgent thrust of his tongue, the rough caress of his hands.

She started to back toward the bed, mouth still locked with Dev's, nearly stumbling in the darkness as she came up hard against the dressing table instead. She gave a gasp of laughter, showering his chin and lightly stubbled cheek with biting little kisses. "I know you've got a bed in here somewhere."

"I have a bed in here somewhere," he groaned, pressing her against the dresser. "Whether we last long enough to get there or not is another thing altogether...."

He moved his hips evocatively against hers, caressing her with his strongly aroused body, and Jess moaned softly. "Hurry," she whispered against his mouth. "Dev, hurry...."

She felt hot and drugged and dizzy, every nerve ending in her body on fire, and she gave another moan as he moved against her again. Her own body responded to that graphic touch so urgently that it made her gasp, the ache between her thighs so explicit and urgent that she was half-wild with it.

She heard her own voice whispering, begging him for the release only he could give her, heard his harsh breathing against her ear, felt his teeth graze her throat as he kissed her roughly. Feeling sanity slip, she sunk her fingers into his hair again and started kissing the strong line of his jaw, his chin, his throat.

He unbuttoned his work shirt impatiently and in the next moment his chest and shoulders were deliciously naked. His skin was hot and salty and she ran her hands over it, wanting to touch him, to hold him, feeling him start with a stifled moan as she caressed his hard nipples with her fingers.

His heart was pounding against her breasts and his breathing was fast and tight as he caressed her urgently, his mouth hot and rough on hers, and then his hand was between them, fumbling with his jeans to free himself. Jess gave a groan of encouragement as he moved against her, steel-in-satin and hard-driving want, and she knew she was going to lose her mind if he didn't hurry.

"Now . . ." she heard herself whisper, her voice an urgent sob of pure need. "Please, Dev . . . now . . . please."

Seven

How Dev managed to wait those few extra moments that it took, he honestly didn't know. But somehow he managed to lever open the top dressing table drawer beside Jess's left hip. The small box of contraceptives was right where he'd put it and he fumbled it open, teeth gritted, breathing a silent prayer of thanks for whatever whim had made him buy them yesterday. He managed to get one out finally and he ripped the protective foil off with his teeth.

"Help me with this," he whispered, guiding Jess's hands.

He groaned as she did just that, hurriedly but competently, just as he'd taught her years ago. And then there was no reality at all beyond the two of them, his own physical desire a fire storm that left him blinded and half-wild with need.

The slender woman in his arms begging him to go on was witch fire and lightning, and he was helpless to deny her. He pulled her nightgown up impatiently, filling his hands with warm female flesh, so ready for her that it was agony just waiting those last few heartbeats until he could slip his hands under her smooth little bottom and lift her urgently.

She was so ready for him that she accepted him fully and easily in one long silken, wet embrace that left him gasping and fighting for control. It tore a soft cry of satisfaction from her and she arched her back, wrapping her legs around his thighs, eyes closed as her head dropped back. She started to move almost at once, urgent and breathless, gripping him fiercely with her thighs, and Dev had to grit his teeth to keep his control from snapping then and there.

A moment or two later she arched back again, bracing her hands on the dressing table behind her, and Dev let his hands slide down the backs of her thighs until he was supporting her weight fully and allowing her to loosen the fierce grip of her legs so he could move more freely.

She gave a gasp as he thrust himself urgently forward and he could see the muscles in her abdomen flex and ripple as she moved in strong counterpoint to his withdrawal, heard her groan softly again as he pressed himself back between her thighs. There was no time to wonder about the miracle of what was happening, no time for anything but the all-encompassing tension that was building like an express train. He moved and kept moving, rhythmically and steadily, listening to her panting little gasps of pleasure and praying he was going to be able to hold on long enough for her.

By some miracle he did, was only half-aware of hearing her give a sharp little cry and arching against him with a sob before he lost it all. He moved against her again and again, fingers tightening on the smooth, taut curves of her bottom, lifting her slightly, pulling her against him. And then that impossible tension within him exploded.

He heard a savage growl of satisfaction and release and realized it was his own voice. Realized, too, that he'd wrenched Jess against him in that last cataclysmic instant and was still holding her fiercely. Gently, he eased her down, letting her slide the length of his body until she was standing unsteadily in front of him. Then, wordlessly, he tossed the rest of their forgotten clothing aside and led her across to the bed, and as he eased himself down under the covers beside her, he found himself wondering if he was going to awaken in the morning and find it had all been a dream.

But she was still there when he awoke a little after two, standing by the window with a blanket draped around her shoulders against the cold, staring out at the sea. He lay there for a long while, saying nothing, content simply to watch her.

It was odd how easily she fit back into his life. It was as though, in some strange way, she'd never been out of it. As though he'd simply been holding a place for her all those years, knowing that one day she'd have to return. If only to fulfill a promise, he reminded himself with a faint smile. She'd been nine and he'd just turned fourteen, and they'd sworn to remain best friends forever. . . .

He eased himself out from under the covers and padded across to where she was standing, wondering if the faint moonlit frown on her face was one of memories, or regret.

She glanced around just then and saw him, and her face broke into a sweet, shy smile. "Hi."

"Hi, yourself," he murmured, slipping both arms around her and kissing the side of her throat. "I woke up lonely."

"Sorry. I got up to check on Heather and got sidetracked by the view."

Dev slipped his hands under the blanket and caressed her warm breasts. They were full and heavy, the tips deliciously soft, and he felt his body respond strongly just to the promise they held.

He whispered something explicit and earthy against her ear and she gave a gentle laugh. "So soon?"

"I think I can find the energy to make it worth your while." He nipped the side of her throat, smiling when he felt her nipples tighten just slightly against his gently caressing hands, knew by the subtle change in her breathing that she was thinking the same thing he was—that it would be long and slow and deep this time, and that before it was over they would both well and truly know the meaning of the word 'satisfaction.'

"Dev..." She frowned slightly, then eased herself away and turned to look at him. She opened her mouth to continue, then hesitated, looking uncomfortable and mildly embarrassed, not meeting his eyes. "I...umm. Damn it, this isn't any of my business and I don't know why I'm asking, but...did you love Laurel Conroy?"

"Love her?" Dev found himself staring at her in surprise. "Of course not. She was just another case. You don't get involved when you're working, you know that."

"Oh." It was a small sound. Thoughtful.

Dev reached out and touched her cheek with the back of his hand. "Did you think...?"

She shrugged, tugging the blanket more tightly around her shoulders, still not looking at him. "You were calling out her name. The other night, when you had that nightmare. And I just wondered..." She shrugged again. "You took her death so hard that I thought...maybe..."

"It wasn't that." It was hard, just getting the words out. And he suddenly realized he had never talked about it—not once—in the entire time since it had happened. "She reminded me of you, if you want the truth. Every time I looked at her, I was seeing you. It—" He bit it off, then drew in a deep breath and said the words aloud. "I think it made me careless. I got so damned wrapped up in the memories and a lot of late-night regrets that I got...sloppy." He heard the tightness in his own voice. "Conroy was good, but not that good. If I'd been doing my job properly, I'd have stopped him cold. Instead, I let him decoy me out of the safe house and when I got back—no more than twenty minutes later—they were all dead. Laurel and her little girl. And Kevin Riley, a rookie who'd been on the force all of six months."

He realized he had his teeth clenched and unlocked his jaw with an effort. "That should have been my first clue that my mind wasn't where it should have been—no one accepts a rookie on a job like that. I should have seen it, Jess. I was a good cop, damn it. I should have *seen* it!''

"You're still a good cop," she said very softly. "But even good cops have cases turn bad on them. And good people die, Dev. You know that. You've seen it before. Faced the senselessness of it before."

"Not like this," Dev whispered, fighting the dark shadows prowling the edges of his mind. "I promised a five-year-old child that I'd keep her safe, Jessie—and I let that monster kill her."

He turned and walked toward the bed, sitting on the edge and staring at the rug between his feet, elbows resting heavily on his knees.

Jess watched him for a moment, then walked across and sat beside him, rubbing his back and shoulders without saying anything. She'd followed the case in the media. Still shivered when she recalled the field day they had with it, TV cameras zooming in for close-ups of Dev's anguished face for the six o'clock highlights, microphones picking up every nuance of rage and helplessness in the grandparents' voices as they'd accused him of negligence.

But only a handful of those same reporters bothered to follow the Internal Affairs Review Board hearing that followed, and even fewer announced that Lieutenant Devlin McAllister had been cleared of any hint of carelessness in the shooting deaths of Laurel Conroy and her five-year-old daughter.

"That's not what made me quit," he suddenly whispered, his voice rough. "It's what happened afterward. After I...caught him."

"Conroy?" Jess frowned. "The reports said you trapped him in that garage down the street, that he fired at you and you fired back. It was just self-defense."

"He didn't fire at me." Dev turned his head to look at her, his eyes as cold as stone. "I found him all right, but he never got a chance to pull the trigger.'' His eyes held hers. ''I murdered a man, Jess. I killed him in cold blood.''

Jess stared at him, fighting a sudden shiver. ''I can't believe that,'' she said very calmly. ''I know you, Dev. You might have *wanted* to, but you couldn't have done it.''

He stared at the floor, a muscle pulsing in his cheek. ''I've tried to convince myself of that a thousand times,'' he whispered. ''But I don't remember him lifting his gun and I don't remember him firing. I just remember the look on his face when I stepped out of the shadows in front of him....''

He shuddered suddenly and buried his face in his hands. ''It's all just a blank, Jess,'' he said in an agonized whisper. ''I try to remember—I've driven myself half-crazy, playing it over and over, trying to remember something that will tell me what happened. But it's always the same. I remember going into the garage, and I remember seeing Conroy crouched by the window. I see his gun—the gun he used to shoot them—and I remember stepping forward and...'' He shook his head, letting it sink even lower, running his fingers through his hair as though he could tear the memories from himself.

''Dev...''

''All I remember is his face in the moonlight.'' His voice was haunted. ''He's looking at me and I can see the fear on him—I can smell it! And the next thing I remember is standing looking down at him, and he's dead. The coroner's report said it was a bullet from my gun...but I don't even remember firing.''

''Dev, the Internal Affairs inquiry was as thorough as they get. *They* say he fired at you and that you killed him in self-defense. They found a slug from his gun in the garage wall right behind where you'd been standing. What more do you need?''

''I need to remember,'' he whispered hoarsely. ''I need to *know*.''

''And that's why you quit the force.''

"How could I ever trust myself again, Jess?" He let his hands drop and sat there, shoulders slumped, face haggard and drawn. "How could anyone else trust me? Every time I drew my weapon, I'd wonder...."

Jess started rubbing his back again, letting the blanket slip to the floor as she knelt on the bed beside him. "It's late, Dev," she said quietly. "Let it go for tonight. Let's just make love and pretend none of the last eight years ever happened, all right?"

He reached for her and drew her down into his arms, sighing as he lay back against the pillows. Cupping her head in his hands, he kissed her deeply and slowly and she could feel the terrible tension in him slowly subside. Then he rolled them both over gently until she was lying beneath him.

Smiling down at her, he smoothed her hair back with his hands. "You're good for me, lady," he whispered, his eyes locked with hers. "You always were. No matter how bad things got, I always knew that if I could just get home to you, everything would be all right."

"And everything's all right now, Dev," she whispered, drawing his mouth down to hers. "Just leave all of it in the past where it belongs and think about today." She moved her hand, hearing the catch in his voice as she touched him gently. "Think about making love to me, Dev," she coaxed. "Think about making it good for me...."

"Look at me," he whispered, cradling her head in his hands. "Look at me, Jessie...."

She had to bite her lip to keep from crying out with pleasure as he pushed himself slowly into the slippery heat of her, watching her face as he sheathed himself fully and completely in her welcoming body. Biting back a moan, she drew her knees up to take him as deeply as she could, knowing he could see her want in her eyes, her need.

"Say my name," he whispered, his fingers flexing in her hair as he moved slowly, erotically between her thighs. "Say my name, Jess—I want you to say it."

"Devlin," she whispered, knowing he needed to hear it. "Only you, Dev. There was never anyone else but you...."

"Say it."

"Dev. Dev..." He needed to know, she realized. Needed to know that it was him she was making love to and not the man who had been between them for eight years.

His eyes burned into her as he eased himself almost free, then moved slowly back, and this time she couldn't stifle the moan. "Dev," she whispered. "Dev..."

She kept whispering it, eyes locked with his, seeing things in their depths that she'd all but forgotten. Seeing the past melt and vanish until it was just the two of them and their soft whispers in the night, knowing that this was, truly, the way it was meant to be.

"Did you sleep in Mr. McAllister's room last night?" Heather looked at Jess curiously, pausing to lick a smear of peanut butter from her hand.

Jess very nearly dropped the spatula in the scrambled eggs. Heather scooped another blob of peanut butter from the jar and smeared it carefully on a piece of toast, and Jess took advantage of her momentary distraction to take a deep breath, trying to retain some semblance of composure.

"I...umm...yes, as a matter of fact, I did," she admitted quite calmly. "We've discussed this kind of thing, Heather. About the feelings a man and a woman can have for each other, I mean." Jess took another deep breath. "About how—"

"Oh, I know all *that*," Heather said with impatience. "I just wish you'd told me, that's all." She put the lid back on the peanut butter jar and gave Jess a look of disapproval. "After all, I tell you where *I'm* going to be. I went into your room in the night to borrow a blanket and I got scared when you weren't there. I *figured* you were with Mr. McAllister, but I think you should tell me these things. 'Specially now, with that Starkey man chasing us."

Jess gave her daughter a startled look, then laughed ruefully. "You're absolutely right, Heather. And I'm sorry. Maybe I should stay in my own room from now on."

"Oh, you don't have to do that," Heather told her with a look of consternation. "I mean, if you really like him and everything, it's okay with me."

Jess smiled, smoothing Heather's thick hair with her hand. "I do like him, Heather," she said quietly. "A lot. And I'm glad you understand."

Heather shrugged casually, biting into the toast and peanut butter. "You could even have another baby, if you want. I wouldn't mind."

Jess was very glad she'd put the spatula down. "I... Well, I appreciate that, Heather, but I wasn't planning on it. Not right now, anyway."

"Oh." Heather nodded, seemingly unperturbed one way or the other. "Okay. Can I go out and play?"

"I... Yes, that's fine." Jess was gratified at how calm she sounded. Bemused, she watched as Heather bounced across the kitchen and out the door with Teddy on her heels. "What an absolutely incredible child...."

"Who?" Dev's husky baritone wrapped around her as he slipped an arm around her waist and kissed the back of her neck.

"My daughter," Jess said with a laugh. "She floors me sometimes with the things she comes out with."

Dev picked up the knife and licked the peanut butter from it. "What did she hit you with?"

"Permission to sleep with you, for one thing," she told him dryly, smiling at his startled expression. "She even informed me that she wouldn't mind a younger sibling if I were so inclined."

Dev smiled lazily, giving her a peanut-butter-flavored kiss. "I hope you told her there's no chance of *that* happening."

Jess frowned slightly and turned back to the stove, starting to poke absently at the scrambled eggs. "I... I told her I wasn't planning on it."

"Good." Dev grabbed two plates from the cupboard and gently elbowed her aside, taking the spatula from her hand and dividing the golden mound of eggs between them. "How about pouring us some coffee?"

"Dev, have you ever thought about having children? Being a father, I mean?" Jess gave him a sidelong glance as she filled two mugs with steaming coffee.

"Hell, no," he rumbled good-naturedly, sitting down at the table. He scooped up a forkful of eggs and got them halfway to his mouth when he suddenly stopped. Fork poised, he looked at her in concern. "There's no chance, is there? I mean, we *were* careful last night, weren't we? Every time?"

"Every time," Jess assured him, forcing herself to smile. "For a man who supposedly lives a hermit's existence, you're well stocked up for situations like that."

He chewed the eggs, looking mildly embarrassed. "Actually, I picked them up a couple of days ago when I was in town. No reason," he added quickly, looking up at her. "I mean, I wasn't *planning* on anything happening between us. But after the other night in the kitchen, I figured it might be an idea to have something on hand. Just in case...."

Jess had to smile. "Yes, you always did take the concept of police protection pretty seriously—even in the bedroom."

Dev shrugged a little too casually. "My mother had to marry my old man when she was sixteen because she was pregnant and her parents kicked her out. Mary waited until she was nineteen, at least, but it still didn't save her from a bad marriage. Donna didn't fall for the marriage part, but she's raising two kids alone." He looked up at her, eyes serious. "When you grow up in a houseful of sisters, you pick up a thing or two. What an unplanned pregnancy can do to a woman's life is one of them."

Jess simply nodded. Then she sat down across from Dev and took a deep breath. "There's something we have to talk about, Dev. About... why I married Gary."

"Hell, Jess, you don't have to explain that," he said quietly. "Loving me was the biggest mistake you ever made. I was everything you didn't need in a man, let's face it. It's no big mystery why you finally got tired of waiting and left—the only question is why it took you so long."

"I was pregnant." In the sudden, electric stillness that followed, Jess could hear her own heart pounding. She swallowed, staring down into her coffee mug, her knuckles white where she was gripping it. She forced herself to relax her fingers, terrified to look at him for fear of what she might see.

"Nearly two months," she went on desperately, as much to fill the silence as to explain. "I couldn't tell you. I knew you'd think I'd done it on purpose to coerce you into marrying me."

"What are you telling me, Jess?" Dev's voice was soft. Much too soft.

Hesitantly, Jess lifted her gaze to meet his. "Heather is your daughter, Dev," she said calmly.

Dev heard the words all right, but they were distant, empty. Almost meaningless. The refrigerator motor suddenly cut in, humming quietly behind him, and he concentrated on the sound, trying to ignore the import of what Jess was saying.

"I couldn't believe it when the doctor told me," Jess said in a whisper. "We'd always been so careful that I—I knew he had to be wrong. So I went to another doctor, sure the test would be negative. But it wasn't...."

Dev could hear her swallow. "I spent the next couple of weeks in a daze, certain it was just a mistake. But the longer I waited, the more I knew it had to be true. I was terrified to tell you. I knew you wouldn't believe for a minute that I hadn't done it on purpose, that I wasn't trying to trick you into marrying me."

"So you married Gary." Dev didn't even bother keeping the anger out of his voice. "Did he know?"

"Of course he knew." Jess looked up at him. "Do you think I'd have married him without telling him that?"

"I don't know why the hell not," he replied heatedly, his stomach twisted into a hard, tight knot of resentment. "You never bothered telling me—and I was the damned father!"

Jess slammed the mug down, scooping her hair back with both hands. "Damn it, Devlin, I don't want this to turn into a shouting match. I'm trying to explai—"

"Don't you think it's a little late for explanations?" Dev lunged to his feet, sending the wooden chair flying. He raked his hand through his hair. "Seems to me everyone in town knew you were carrying my baby but me."

"You didn't want to know!" Jess was on her feet in the next instant in a swirl of glistening hair and angry eyes. "Every time I mentioned marriage or anything else even remotely associated with settling down, you broke into a cold sweat. You'd twist everything around until we'd wind up fighting—it was your way of protecting yourself. Your way of keeping me from getting too close."

Her dark eyes flashed. "That last night, Dev—that was the night I'd planned to tell you. I'd managed to get the topic around to marriage—naively thinking that maybe you'd mellowed since the last time we'd talked about it—and we wound up in the worst fight we'd ever had. When you went storming out, I didn't even expect to see you again. I went over to Gary's—I told him about the baby then, Dev. *That's* why he was holding me when you came bursting in—because I was pregnant and crying my eyes out because I thought I'd lost you for good."

"You never said a damned thing that night about a baby."

"You didn't give me a chance!" She glared across the room at him, her cheeks flushed with anger. "You came roaring into Gary's apartment like a tornado and saw him sitting on the sofa with his arms around me, and in the next instant you'd punched him in the mouth and were telling me to get my things out of *your* apartment. Then you went slamming out again, and the next thing I heard you'd left town.''

Dev's lip curled. "And a week later you married Gary."

"I didn't think you were coming back!"

"You didn't even love him."

"It didn't matter!" Jess faced him angrily, fists clenched, twin spots of color glowing high on her cheekbones. "All that mattered was making sure my baby had a father! And a home, Devlin. A normal, stable home!"

Her eyes glittered with sudden tears, and Dev's stomach gave a sharp twist at the anguish and sudden fury on her pale face. "I let you talk me into moving in with you because I loved you so much I couldn't think straight. And then I watched myself becoming more and more like my mother with every week that went by, waiting...always waiting."

"You knew how I felt about marriage before you moved in," Dev said between gritted teeth.

"I know that," she said more quietly. "But the day I found out I was pregnant, I panicked. All I could see was my mother sitting by that damned telephone day after day, waiting for him to call, so caught up in her own unhappiness and silly dreams that she never had any time for *me*. I could not let that happen to a child of mine, Dev. Gary told me he'd marry me, and I agreed."

Dev found himself simply staring at her, his anger and resentment a seething hot mass burning his gut. He'd hated Gary for marrying Jess, found him hating the man a little more in that moment for having not only the woman, but the child, as well. And all those years of happiness that by rights had been his.

"You had no right," he said hoarsely. "She was my daughter, not Elliott's. You had no right to keep her from me."

"I did the best I could with what I had!" It was almost a cry, the pain in it so real he could see it in her eyes. "Don't

you dare make me into the culprit in this, Devlin Mc-
Allister! Maybe I was wrong—maybe I should have given
you a chance—but I didn't. I was pregnant, I was scared and
all I wanted was someone to hold me and tell me it was going
to be all right.''

"And good ol' Gary was in the right place at the right
time," Dev drawled sarcastically. "Not that he needed to
think twice. Hell, he always wanted you, Jess. He must have
thought he'd died and gone to heaven to wind up not only
with Dev McAllister's woman, but Dev McAllister's kid,
too!"

"My God, Dev, he worshiped the ground you walked
on." Her voice broke on a sob of laughter. "The only reason he became a cop was because it was your dream and he
wanted to share it. He'd have died for you if he—" She
stopped abruptly, then her face crumpled slightly, filled with
pain. "Oh, damn," she whispered, putting her hand out as
though to touch him. "Oh, Dev, I'm sorry. That was a stupid thing to say. I didn't mean—"

"Say it!" Dev lashed out savagely. His blood was
pounding in his temples and he could feel the helpless rage
welling up through him, could see Gary's eyes in the moonlight, could hear the sound of a gunshot.... "Say it! I killed
him, Jess. I killed your husband!"

"Dev...!"

He spun away from her outstretched hand and stumbled
out the back door, half-blinded by what he could have
sworn were tears if he didn't know better. She called his
name but he ignored her, kept walking fast and hard until
he'd put the sound of her voice behind him, could hear
nothing but the roar of the sea and screaming gulls.

But even they didn't blot out the other sound. The one
inside his skull: the sound of a high-powered rifle shot slic-
ing through the night, the sound of it hitting flesh, the sound
of Gary's last tortured breath as he'd bled his life away on

that deserted dock while Dev had crouched beside him, begging him to hang on.

He couldn't possibly stay out there all night.

Jess leaned against the sink, a cup of untasted tea in her hand, and stared out into the darkness beyond the window.

He was still there, standing in his work shed stripping down a small outboard engine, spotlighted by the single light bulb hanging from the ceiling. He'd been out there for nearly three hours now, and before that he'd chopped another half cord of wood, wielding the ax with a single-minded purposefulness bordering on fury.

She started to go out to him a number of times, but had managed to catch herself. He had to work it through alone, finding whatever answers made any sense to him. Just as she had, finally, found the ones she needed.

It was hours later that she heard him come in. She listened to his footsteps as he walked down the corridor toward his bedroom. They paused in front of the door to her room and Jess held her breath. But he didn't come in. The footsteps resumed after a long while, and she eased her breath out again, both relieved and disappointed.

It seemed to go on for hours, that restless pacing just beyond her door. She'd doze off and awaken a while later to hear him still out there, prowling the shadows of his lair like some great wounded beast, too proud to ask for help, too fearful of capture to risk letting anyone get too near.

They wove themselves into her dreams, those footsteps, until she couldn't tell sleep from wakefulness, pursuer from pursued. And she awoke once near dawn to find him beside her.

Fully clothed, he was lying on his back on top of the bedspread, his unshaven cheeks gaunt with exhaustion, staring at the ceiling. One hand lay on her pillow, as though he'd reached toward her but hadn't wanted to waken her, and she moved her own to cover it.

He didn't look at her, didn't make any sign at all that he knew she was awake except to tighten his fingers fiercely around hers. But he seemed to relax slightly, and a few minutes later he let his eyes slide closed and after a while she heard his breathing deepen as he slipped into sleep.

Eight

————

He stood at the sliding glass doors leading out to what would be a pine deck if he ever got around to finishing it, and watched his daughter play.

His daughter.

Dev let the words linger in his mind. They'd been unfamiliar at first, almost frightening, but for the last couple of hours he'd been almost teasing himself with them, enjoying the sound.

It had been unimaginable at first. He'd stormed out of the house certain that Jess had been lying to him, using the myth of fatherhood to pay him back for walking out on her eight years ago. But even as he'd said the words to himself, he'd known that she hadn't been lying at all. That she well and truly had been pregnant with his child, had been alone and scared and thinking herself abandoned. Had turned to the only other person she knew would help her.

For a few hours yesterday, he'd managed to hate Gary. His anger had been deep and bitter as he'd thought of how

Gary had stepped in and taken what wasn't his to take—not just Jessie, but the child, as well. Dreams. A future. A family.

All the things, Dev realized, that he'd never thought he'd have himself. He'd missed seven years of his daughter's life, and even more than seven years with Jess, loving her, sharing all those things married people share.

He could remember how he'd driven by their house late at night sometimes when he couldn't sleep. He'd sit in the car, alone and chilled, and try to imagine them in there, wrapped in each other's arms. Loving each other. Sharing laughter and small talk and the daily humdrum chores. Making plans. Going shopping. Watching TV in the evening and eating buttered popcorn out of the same big bowl.

His feelings of loneliness and despair, of being left out of the threesome they'd once been, would leave him aching for hours afterward, sometimes even days. And now to find that they'd been sharing something much more precious...

He became aware suddenly that Jess was standing in the doorway of the living room, caught there as though she'd stepped into the room before realizing he was there. Without turning around, he said, "Does she know?"

There was a wary silence. "I...don't think so." Her voice sounded rough. Almost as though she'd been crying.

He glanced around at her. She didn't say anything, just stood there watching him, looking small and oddly defenseless. And suddenly, he realized what it must have cost her to come here.

"Why, Jess?" He held her gaze, searching her dark eyes for something he could understand. "Why bother telling me at all? Odds are I never would have found out."

She managed a rough smile, rubbing her arms as though chilled, and walked slowly toward him. "Why not ask me something simple, like the principle of nuclear fission or differential calculus?" Then she let the smile fade and looked out to where Heather, Chris and Pud were playing catch. "That's not much of an answer, I guess."

"It's not any answer," Dev said irritably, wishing he understood even half of what was going on. Life had been fairly simple until yesterday.

"I never knew my father, Dev. And I don't want that to happen to Heather. She needs to feel... connected. Part of something. I never had that. There was always a part of me that wasn't there. I don't want her growing up knowing that kind of emptiness."

"She had Gary," he said thickly.

"Gary couldn't do it. He tried—in his own way, he was a good husband and a good father—but he never had your kind of strength. Heather does. She's a part of you. And I think she should know you."

"Did you love him?" He hadn't wanted to ask the question, hating his own weakness for needing to know.

"Not the way I loved you, Dev," she said quietly. "Gary was good to me... at least he tried to be when he wasn't drinking or strung out. And he did love me. There have been worse marriages."

"At least he was there for you when you needed him," he said raggedly. "Damn it, Jess, it was more than I gave you."

"You gave me Heather," she said very softly, putting her hand on his arm. "As long as I had her, I had a part of you."

"If I'd been there for you, none of this would have happened. All you ever wanted was a nice, comfortable marriage, Jess—and I put you through hell because I was too scared to admit I needed you."

"We weren't ready." She looked at him evenly. "We would have wound up hating each other, Dev. You would have felt trapped and smothered, and I'd have resented your anger. Pretty soon it would have just unraveled."

Then she smiled faintly and looked out at Heather. "Besides, it made me strong. I had to be hit over the head a few times before I caught on, but I finally realized that the only person responsible for making me happy is me."

"And your forever man?"

She gave a quiet laugh. "Oh, maybe he's out there some-where. If he is, I'll find him one day. But the nice thing is that I don't *need* him anymore." She let her smile widen, glancing sidelong at him. "Besides, Dev, I'll always have you."

For some reason, it made his heart give a little twist, hearing her come out and say it like that. *I'll always have you.*

He nodded, not saying anything, and stared out at the kids. They'd scrounged up a bat from somewhere and were setting out bases, a process that seemed to require a lot of shouting and arguing. "That could be us out there about twenty years ago," he said suddenly. "Remember when you nailed that homer off the end of the bat and split it clean in two?"

"And broke Joey Mendez's nose into the bargain. You and Gary stuck a handful of mud onto it to stop the bleed-ing, and we just kept on playing." She grinned suddenly. "I saw Joey at Gary's funeral. He's an attorney in some big-deal downtown law office, and his nose still has that weird little bend in it. You'd think he'd have had it fixed by now."

"Maybe he likes the memories it brings," he said softly.

Jess simply nodded, smiling reminiscently.

"I was there the night Gary died."

"Yes, I know." Dev looked at her in surprise and she shrugged. "Well, not all of it, probably. I know you'd ar-ranged to meet him that night. That someone was waiting for you and..." She paused for just an instant, a flicker of pain crossing her face. "That Gary was shot and killed." She looked up at him. "The report said he died quickly—and that you were there with him at the last. I was always thankful for that. That he didn't die with strangers."

Dev gritted his teeth. "He wouldn't have died at all if it hadn't been for me," he said tightly. "When Gary's name came up during the investigation, I couldn't believe my luck. I wanted him so bad I could taste it." He paused, trying to figure out how to explain what had happened next. "But...I couldn't do it. In the end, he was still my oldest friend. I wanted to get him out of it before the roof caved in and he got buried alive.''

Jess didn't say anything, but her smile did. And her eyes, warm with gratitude and what a man who still believed in dreams might mistake for love.

"I met him that night to convince him to give me everything he had on the people who were involved, especially Starkey. And I think he'd have done it, Jess. He was scared by then. Cocky as hell, of course, but he'd finally realized how much trouble he was in. But before he could tell me anything useful, there was a gunshot...and he went down.''

"Someone knew Gary was meeting you and followed him."

"I should have anticipated it," he grated. "That's half of what being a cop is about, being able to outthink the opposition. The point is, I didn't take even the simplest precautions. And I can't help wondering..." He drew in a deep breath. "It's haunted me for two years now, Jess. That perhaps my obsession with bringing Starkey down was just a cover-up for my real motives. That maybe I was after Gary all the time.''

"I don't believe that any more than I believe you could have killed Martin Conroy in cold blood," Jess said softly. "You may have hated Gary for a while after he married me, but there's no way you would have hurt him. My God, Dev, you loved him like a brother. We both did.''

"I wish I could be so sure," Dev said wearily. He braced his arm on the door frame and leaned against it, staring out at Heather and the two boys. "I broke the first rule of being a good cop, Jess. I let my feelings get in the way of common sense. He'd probably be alive right now if I'd kept my mind on business.''

"You don't know that. Gary was...Gary. He lived his whole life out there on the edge, Dev. Maybe he wouldn't have died that night, but who's to know about the night after that? Or the next? The point is, you tried to help him because he was your friend.''

Dev glanced down at her. The sky was overcast, threatening rain, yet a stray sunbeam had chosen that moment to break through. It cascaded around her, making her glossy dark hair glow, and he felt his stomach constrict as it did every time he found himself close to her. Had he deliberately lured Gary to that dock, knowing someone would be waiting for them? With Gary gone, Jess would be free...free for the taking.

He forced himself to look away. Or maybe, as she said, it was the caring that did it. ''The point is, trying to help got him killed. Like I said, I let my feelings get in the way.''

Feelings. Jess looked at Dev thoughtfully, wondering what was going on behind those silvery gray eyes. As always, he kept that part of himself—the feeling part—tightly closed off, afraid of giving too much of himself away, of making himself vulnerable. He was tearing himself up inside with guilt...the fear that he had cared too much or hadn't cared enough. Either way, Gary was dead and he was alive.

''Is that why you've never gotten in touch with me since Gary's death?'' she asked quietly. ''Why you jeopardized your career to make sure his pension and insurance were reinstated? Because of guilt?''

His profile was like stone against the glass, eyes slightly narrowed, jaw firm.

But she didn't have to hear him say it to know it was true. He'd stayed away because he couldn't look her in the eye, believing himself to be responsible for her husband's death. And then she'd turned up here and made those nightmares more real than ever.

She shouldn't have come, Jess realized suddenly. He'd come out here to heal himself as best as he could, and she was just tearing all those old wounds open again. And she had no right. No right at all.

She took a deep breath, knowing in that instant what she had to do. "I'm leaving tomorrow."

She turned and walked across to the coffee table, starting to pick up the scattered magazines and books. The ID bracelet was still where he'd tossed it that first day and she picked it up, running her thumb idly over the engraving. Then she put it carefully down and straightened, finding Dev looking at her with an odd expression.

"You're safer here." He walked toward her, brows tugged together.

"I can do this on my own, Devlin," she said firmly. "It wasn't right to come running to you, expecting you to drop everything to take care of me. That was fine when I was ten years old, but we're not kids anymore. And Rich Starkey isn't the schoolyard bully."

"Jess—" Dev's eyes narrowed slightly.

"We'll work something out about Heather later—visitation rights, I mean. I don't know how she'll take the news about your being her father, but I'm certain once the surprise has worn off, she'll want to spend some time with you. I hope you'll at least think about it." She held his gaze evenly. "For your sake, Dev, as well as hers. I think you could use someone...." *Someone to love you,* she finished silently, deciding it was probably more prudent not to say it aloud.

"But there is one thing I want you to do for me." She took another deep breath. "Dev, I want you to keep Heather. For a while, anyway. I want to know that if something happens to me, she'll be safe. And I don't want my mother to get custody. She can barely take care of herself, let alone a seven-year-old."

Dev felt himself go cold. He eased his breath out very carefully. "What the hell are you talking about?"

"Just until I get this mess with Starkey straightened out. Besides, it will give you a chance to get to know each other."

Something cold was gnawing at his gut and he had a flash image of wide blue eyes. Trusting eyes.... "Get serious,

Jess! Do I look like someone who knows how to take care of a seven-year-old kid?''

"You're going to have to," she said very calmly. "I can't do this and worry about Heather, too, Dev. I think you owe me this much at least."

"I don't owe you a damned thing," he ground out. "You were the one who ran off and married Gary without even telling me you were pregnant."

"Dev," she said in a low, urgent voice, "I *need* you to keep her safe for me. Please...!"

"I can't do it!" He wheeled around to face her. "I don't want the damned responsibility, don't you get it? I'm sick and tired of having people depend on me to keep them safe, then having them die! I don't want you, and I don't want her!"

He shouldered by her and strode out of the room, fighting the sickness clawing at him, trying not to think of all those hopeful, trusting faces. Gary. Laurel Conroy. A five-year-old girl with eyes the color of forget-me-nots.

He was standing in his workshop when she came out, reassembling the small outboard engine he'd stripped apart the previous day. She stood in the doorway, hands tucked in the pockets of her khaki slacks, watching him silently.

"I'm sorry," he said gruffly. "I didn't mean...that."

"I know I'm asking a lot."

"It's not that. It's..." He tossed the wrench down and wiped his hands on a rag, turning to look at her. "Hell, Jess, you saw the kind of shape I was in when you got here. Would you trust the man you hauled out of that ditch the other morning with your own daughter?"

"I'd trust that man with my life."

It wasn't what he wanted to hear. *Trust me,* he'd told Shelley Conroy. *Trust me, and I'll keep you safe....*

A little shiver wound its way slowly down his spine and he turned back to the workbench. "I'm not the man you need, Jess," he said hoarsely. "I'm burned-out and worn up...there just isn't anything left anymore. I don't want any more blood on my hands.''

"I don't think that's what you're scared of at all," Jess said softly. "I think you're afraid of caring too much, just like you always were. Afraid of letting someone too close."

"Maybe I am," he said in a rough voice. "Or maybe I'm just tired of getting torn up inside every time something goes wrong."

"How would you know, Dev?" she challenged angrily. "You've never let it get that far!"

Dev looked around, but she was already striding away, her back straight. Then, suddenly she paused. Turned to look at him, dark eyes holding the glitter of what he could have sworn were tears. "I managed to convince myself that you stayed away after Gary died because you were afraid I wouldn't still want you. But now I realize you stayed away because you were afraid I would." She tried to laugh, but it sounded more like a sob. "You know, Dev, it's not loving someone that's the hard part. It's loving someone who can't love you back."

"Damn it, Jess—"

But she turned and kept walking, and Dev subsided after a moment, not even knowing what he'd been going to say.

It was an odd feeling, waking up a father.

This was the second morning in a row that the realization of that fact hit him just as he opened his eyes, and he still wasn't entirely sure he was comfortable with it. There was a sense of permanence to it he'd never anticipated, a feeling of . . . hell, of completeness.

It wasn't just him anymore. There was Jess, and there was the child that they had created together. They were linked now in ways he only half understood, he and Jess and the dark-haired girl who was his daughter, and he'd never again be just one man, alone and isolated in his world.

And he wasn't sure he liked the feeling.

Scrubbing at his sleep-tousled hair, Dev sat up and looked at the digital clock on the bedside table, swearing under his breath as he realized how late it was. He'd tossed and turned half the night, as usual, although once he had fallen asleep he'd stayed that way, his night undisturbed by demons.

He got up and headed for the bathroom, hearing the clatter of cutlery and dishes coming from the kitchen, and as he stepped under the pounding hot spray of the shower, he found himself smiling.

That was something else he'd gotten used to a damned sight quicker than he'd ever anticipated—having a woman around all the time. Except it wasn't just any woman, he corrected as he lathered himself with soap. It was Jess.

He was still contemplating this as he pulled on his jeans and a clean cotton shirt. It was comfortable, having her here. He preferred waking up and finding her beside him, all warm and velvet-soft and naked, but even just knowing she was somewhere in the house felt good.

Which wasn't the way it was supposed to be at all.

No illusions this time, he told himself bitterly as he met his own eyes in the mirror above the dressing table. Her being here didn't signal a new beginning; if anything, it was just the tying up of old loose ends so they could both get on with their lives. She'd said as much yesterday.

Heather looked up as he came into the kitchen. She was kneeling on a chair that she'd drawn up in front of the stove, and was pouring puddles of batter onto the pancake griddle. Except that she'd missed a time or two, Dev noticed, and she, the front of the stove, the counter and the floor were covered with it, as well. Teddy was half under the chair, licking batter off the floor and the stove front, and he wriggled back out after a moment, looking pleased with himself, his nose and muzzle dusted with flour.

"I hope you like pancakes." She caught her tongue between her teeth as she unsteadily dribbled the last of the batter out of the sticky bowl. "Some of them are cooked a little too much, but they taste okay."

Dev looked at the pile of pancakes stacked on a plate beside Heather's elbow. "Just coffee," he muttered, reaching for a mug. "You always make this kind of mess when you cook?"

"Are you always this grumpy in the morning?" she shot back with a mildly hostile look. "I can't help it if I make a mess. I'm only seven. But you don't have to worry. I'll clean it up."

Put firmly in his place, Dev retreated to the table with his coffee. Heather ignored him, her back as stiff as only Jess Elliott's offspring could make it. And his, too, he reminded himself with a hint of what he suddenly realized was paternal pride. In fact it was probably a toss-up as to which half—Jess's or his own—was responsible for the jut of that stubborn little chin.

"I'm...uh...sorry," he muttered.

"You don't *have* to like me, you know." Heather turned the pancakes inexpertly, managing to drop only one down the front of the stove. It slithered messily to the floor where Teddy downed it in a single gulp.

"I like you fine," he growled, deciding there was more to this fathering business than met the eye. "What makes you think I don't?"

"You don't act as though you like me," she replied bluntly.

Dev winced. It was like dealing with a diminutive version of Jess herself—ask her a question and you got an answer, whether you liked it or not. She even had the same way of looking you straight in the eye when she said it. "I'm just not used to having kids around, that's all," he muttered, stirring sugar into his coffee. "And things are a little complicated right now."

"You mean about you being my father?"

It startled Dev so badly that he managed to spill his coffee, and he swore under his breath as he mopped it up. "How the hell—heck do you know that?"

She shrugged carelessly. "Oh, I heard Mom and Grandma Weston talking about it one day. A long time ago."

"Does your mother know you know?"

"Nope." Heather slid off the chair and carried the bowl across to the sink. "I think she wanted to see if you an' her got along okay before she told me. Just in case you told us to go away or something. That way I wouldn't be too disappointed."

"I . . . see." Dev eyed her small straight back. "So you're not, then? Disappointed, I mean."

"Well . . ." Heather turned and gave him a speculative look. "It's too soon to say for sure or not. You don't make a very good first impression, though, do you?"

It stung more than it probably should have and he gave her a sharp look, wondering if all seven-year-olds were this precocious, or if he'd just lucked out. "I wasn't expecting company," he told her testily, rummaging through the clutter on the table for his cigarettes. "If you turn up on someone's doorstep without an invitation, you take what you get."

"If you had a phone," she advised him just as testily, "it wouldn't have been a surprise, would it?"

"I don't have a phone because I don't like visitors."

"Do you always drink so much?"

Dev had his mouth open for an irate reply when he caught himself. Frowning, he stared at Heather's back as she scrubbed at the spilled batter, wondering how old she'd been when Jess left Gary. Three maybe? Almost four? Old enough to know a drunk when she saw him. Old enough to know she didn't like it.

He hadn't been much older himself when he'd learned firsthand what living with a drunkard was like. All he had to do was close his eyes and he could still see his father's face, distorted with liquor and rage, shoved close to his, his breath reeking of cheap whiskey, his eyes bloodshot and bleary.

"No," he said quietly, shoving the memory away. "That was only the second time in my life, Heather. And the last."

Heather nodded with satisfaction. Then she saw the pack of cigarettes in Dev's hand, and her small mouth pursed with disapproval. Sighing, Dev tossed them aside. "Satisfied?"

She nodded again, smiling a bit shyly. "Grandma Weston says I'm bossy, but Mom says I just have forthright opinions."

"Yeah, I can see your mother saying something like that," Dev said with a snort of laughter. "She's had a few of her own over the years."

"She says you're hard to get along with because you don't like people getting too close. She says you find it hard to let people love you. That you're scared of imit . . . inimit . . ."

"Intimacy?" Dev offered darkly.

Heather nodded. "She says that every time you loved someone and showed it, you got hurt—so now you don't want to show it." Brown eyes met his, slightly accusing, slightly assessing. "She *says* you don't know what's good for you most of the time."

"Oh, she does, does she?"

"Yep. She says you need one good woman and a bunch of kids to show you that being married doesn't have to be a . . . a war zone, I think she called it. That love doesn't have to hurt."

"Your mother's a real whiz on the subject of one Devlin McAllister, isn't she?" Dev muttered, pouring himself another cup of coffee. "Where is she, anyway?"

"Gone."

Dev looked up sharply. "What do you mean, gone? Where?"

"Into town. She said she was going to check the ferry schedule to go back home this afternoon."

"Damn!" Why it caught him by surprise, he had no idea. She'd already told him that she was going back. But underneath he'd hoped . . .

Hoped what, he asked himself savagely. That the other night in bed meant more than it had? That she'd settle for another day-to-day relationship with him as she had eight years ago, with no commitment, no promises, no future?

She wasn't that twenty-one-year-old college kid anymore, full of dreams of what love meant instead of the reality. She was a grown woman with a child, a widow of two years who had put her life in order, had built up her own business, her own future. The last damned thing she needed was a burned out ex-cop so haunted by the past he couldn't even get through a full night without coming up out of a nightmare screaming.

As much as he liked having her here, as good as it would be to have her stay, he didn't have the right to ask, he realized that now. No right to make her hope for things he doubted he'd ever be able to give her. He could probably do it—persuade her to stay with him. He had once, holding her with the promises of dreams.

And he'd damned near broken her heart. He couldn't do that again. Not to Jessie. She was too important to him. She deserved someone as special as she was, someone who could love her as much as she deserved to be loved, who could open his heart and take all she had to give. And whoever he was, he'd be damned lucky to have a woman like her. Luckier than most men could even dream of being. And if he hurt her, Dev found himself thinking, eyes narrowing, he'd have Devlin McAllister to answer to....

"Hey, here comes Frankie Hudson."

Dev shook off his brooding thoughts and looked out the screen door to see Frankie's old green truck jitterbugging down the lane, raising a smoky trail of dust. He grunted and downed his coffee in one swallow, then got to his feet. She'd come for her outboard motor, probably, and he'd been so damned distracted these past few days he hadn't finished putting it together.

"Can I stay with you?"

The question caught Dev just as he was going to push the screen door open. He looked around at Heather. "I'm not going anywhere—just out to get Frankie's outboard."

"I didn't mean that." She frowned, her small heart-shaped face going very serious as she walked slowly across to look up at him. "I mean after."

"After?"

"After Mom goes back to Seattle. Can I stay here on Whiskey Island with you? Just until school starts...."

She gazed up at him so hopefully that Dev's stomach gave a little twist. "I'm not really set up here to take care of a kid," he said quietly. "You'd get bored in no time, and—"

"No, I wouldn't," she assured him swiftly. "Chris and Pud live right next door, and there's Frankie and lots of other people. I wouldn't be any trouble, promise. I can take care of myself. And I can do stuff for you. I don't cook very well yet, but I can keep the house tidy and take Teddy for walks and I can even do the laundry... although sometimes I need help sorting. I can make the beds and... and help you go shopping and everything."

There was something in those wide brown eyes that caught at Dev in a way he'd never felt before and he found himself hesitating. "I doubt your mother would go for it...."

Hope sparkled in her eyes. "But if she said it was okay, you'd let me stay for the summer, right?"

Common sense said it was impossible. Hell, he didn't know the first thing about being a father. And the *last* thing he needed was a seven-year-old girl underfoot all summer, getting in the way and driving him crazy with her questions and her 'forthright opinions.' He'd have to watch his language and wear pants when he was in his own damned house and she'd probably expect him to read to her at night and help her with her hair and all the rest of it. It was sheer insanity to even consider it.

And yet he heard himself saying, "We'll see."

Her face broke into a smile that lit up the entire room and Dev felt that little tug again. She looked so much like Jess at that age that he had a moment of displaced time, suddenly twelve years old himself again, the world a place of unlimited possibilities.

"I didn't say it was final," he said gruffly, pushing the door open. "I just said we'll see."

Frankie was striding across the yard toward him, flyaway strands of gray hair sticking out from under her cap like radar antennae. "Thought I'd better get out here to tell you," she said before she was even halfway across the yard. "That guy you were keeping an eye out for? Well, he's here. Fella who owns the car place said he rented a blue Le Baron to some guy callin' himself Martin Conroy. Except he matched the description that— You okay, McAllister?"

Dev nodded, his mind still reeling. The name had sent an instinctive jolt of horror through him so strong he could still taste it, adrenaline starting to pump even as his brain was telling him that what he'd heard was impossible.

Conroy was as dead as they come. As dead as the wife and five-year-old daughter he'd murdered.

What had made Starkey use *that* particular name? A warning? Or just his perverse way of taunting the man who'd put him in prison for two long years? The man who was now between him and what he wanted.

Shaken, Dev nodded again. "When? Where?"

"This morning, early. Nobody's seen him since."

"Tulley know?"

"Yep. He figured you'd want to know pronto."

"Thanks, Frankie." Dev drew in a deep breath, trying to quiet his hammering heart. He wet his lips and looked around, eyes narrowing. "He'll come here for her." Except Jess wasn't here. She was in town, and she'd come driving back unsuspecting, with Starkey somewhere out there looking for her. "Frankie, I need your help."

"Name it."

"Take Heather back to your place. Or better yet, get on that boat of yours and hightail it to somewhere safe."

"Good as done."

Dev turned and started back to the house, Frankie plodding along beside him. "Jess went in to town—odds are she doesn't know he's on the island yet, and I don't want her driving back here alone in case he's got the road staked out."

"You go after your lady. I'll take care of the youngster."

Dev was just reaching for the door when it opened and Heather came out, grinning at Frankie. "Heather," he said quietly, "something's come up and I have to go into town. I want you to go home with Frankie, and I want you to do everything she tells you, okay?"

Heather's smile vanished and she looked up at Dev with wide, frightened eyes. "He's here, isn't he?" she whispered. "That man who came to the house and frightened my mom."

"He's here," Dev said grimly. "But there's nothing to worry about. I just want to make sure your mom gets back okay, so I'm going to find her." He looked at Frankie. "You need a gun?"

"Hell, no," she snorted. "My old Winchester can hold off anything as comes at me. You get out there and find your lady."

Dev stepped by Heather and went across to the broom closet, taking down the metal box and unlocking it. Heather and Frankie said nothing, just watching as he loaded the revolver, slid it into his waistband and shoved a box of shells into his hip pocket.

Heather's eyes were huge and dark. "If he finds us, he's going to hurt Mommy and me, isn't he?"

Dev had to grit his teeth, hearing another small, scared voice asking the same thing, seeing another pair of eyes, blue this time, gazing up at him with the same fear in them. "No," he choked out. "He's not going to hurt you. I'm not going to let anything happen to you and your mother, and that's a promise...."

She nodded, smiling a little tentatively, and Dev had to fight to catch his breath, remembering...

He wheeled away and pushed the door open with his shoulder, then glanced around at Frankie. "She's my daughter," he said quietly, the word as warm and sweet on his tongue as melted chocolate. "Jess's and mine..."

"Think I'm blind or somethin'? Knew that the minute I set eyes on her, f'cryin' out loud."

Dev blinked. "You did?"

"A person'd have to be a damned fool not to see it straight off," she said bluntly. "Now get. I'll take care of your daughter for you, you can count on that."

"Be careful...." Heather's eyes held his, filled with worry.

Dev smiled. "I'll be careful, Scout. You just take care of Frankie for me."

Nine

The blue Le Baron was still behind her somewhere.

Jess glanced into the rearview mirror again uneasily, but the narrow dirt road was so winding and hilly, and the cloud of dust her car was raising so thick, that she couldn't see a thing. Just a tantalizing glimpse of blue now and again, the flicker of morning sunlight on chrome or glass as the vehicle crested a hill. Nothing, really, that should be making her this nervous.

Yet she was. Maybe it was just the way it hung back there, never getting any nearer, or maybe it was just her own highly active imagination, but she could swear it was deliberately following her.

Which didn't make any sense at all, she told herself firmly. Unless Dev and Tulley had arranged to have someone keep an eye on her, of course, and hadn't bothered to tell her about it—and she wouldn't put it past either of them. In spite of herself, Jess had to smile. For a man who swore he wasn't a cop anymore, Dev McAllister was certainly *acting* like a cop.

But then, Dev always had been good at acting. He'd spent his entire life pretending not to care, pretending he didn't need anyone, didn't want anyone. But she'd always been able to see through the bluff and protective armor to the real Devlin inside. She'd been the only person he'd ever let that close, and while they'd been kids it hadn't mattered. They'd been best friends, and you can let best friends that close because they'll never betray you.

It's when kids grow into adults that the trouble starts; when best friends turn into lovers that the chance of betrayal is suddenly there. That's what had scared Dev. She'd been his weak spot, the one person who knew Devlin McAllister inside out, and he'd frantically tried to close her out before she could somehow hurt him. Driving her out of his life—and Gary with her—had been the only way he knew to protect himself.

He was doing the same thing now.

Maybe she shouldn't leave, she found herself thinking suddenly. Maybe she should just damned well stay here and make him face it—for Heather's sake, if not for his own. Maybe she was making it too easy for him, giving in without a fight like this. Because Heather *deserved* a chance to know him.

Jess's eyes narrowed slightly. She had never known the man who'd been her father. Oh, she knew his name and what he looked like, but she'd never *known* him. Presents had appeared punctually on her birthday and at Christmas, and when she'd needed braces or new shoes, the money had been there—as it had been when she'd decided to go to college.

But of all the things he could have given her, money was the least important. What she'd wanted was a hug now and again. What she'd wanted was a father to take her down to the schoolyard and push her on a swing like the other fathers did, a father to stand up and applaud at the school play, to walk beside her on a sunny afternoon, hand in hand, and tell her things.

But that part of him—the loving, sharing part—had belonged to his other children. His "real" children, as she still thought of them. Two girls, one a year older than Jess, the other a couple of years younger, and a boy. She'd never met them, knew only that she had three half siblings somewhere in the world who shared some of the same blood.

It had always been an odd feeling, and she still found herself looking at strangers on the street and wondering—

The Le Baron came roaring out of the cloud of dust behind her like a juggernaut, startling her so badly she nearly steered her car straight into the ditch. It filled her rearview mirror and for an instant she thought it was going to hit her, then it veered out and around and she gave a gasp of relief, her heart pounding so hard she felt light-headed.

She eased off the accelerator to let it pass, swearing under her breath with delayed shock—as annoyed at the other driver for choosing this particular stretch of road to go by her as at her own inattention. The road here was narrow and winding as it ran through heavy forest, the sun all but blocked by the tall pine and fir trees looming to either side.

But the other car didn't pass. It pulled even with her and then, suddenly, it jerked sideways and hit the side of her car so hard that Jess nearly lost the wheel. She gave a gasp of shock as her shoulder harness snapped tight, keeping her from being thrown forward, and she fought for control as her small rental slewed dangerously. She had no time to think, no time to even be properly afraid, and then the big Chrysler was coming in again.

She was braced for it this time, but it was too late. The other car, bigger and more powerful, simply bulldozed her off the road and she swore breathlessly, feeling the wheel catch in the soft shoulder and knowing there wasn't a thing she could do.

The steering wheel wrenched out of her hands and she felt the car start to go, knew with a kind of weary despair that

it was going to roll. She covered her face with her arms as it
started to lift, and then she was flung against the shoulder
harness so hard it knocked her breath from her and she felt
the car start to go over. . . .

Something was wrong.

Dev swore and slammed his open palm against the steering wheel in frustration. She couldn't have just disappeared, damn it!

Jess hadn't been in to check the ferry schedule, the people in the office were certain of that, and he'd been to every
marina and charter boat captain in town and had gotten the
same story. No one had talked with her, or even seen her.

It didn't make any sense. Dev scrubbed his fingers
through his hair, swearing again. She'd left his place nearly
two hours ago. Why was it taking her so long to make a
thirty-minute drive?

Unless something had happened. She could have had a
flat, or engine trouble. She could be out there right now on
any of a dozen of the narrow dirt roads that crisscrossed the
island, trying to change a balky tire. Or she could have had
an accident . . . run off the road, hit a deer. She could have
stopped to talk with someone, or look at the scenery— Hell,
knowing Jess, she could be out there somewhere picking
flowers!

He raked his hair back again and turned the key in the
truck ignition. Maybe his best bet was simply to go home
and wait for her. He'd find Tulley and have him keep an eye
out for her, maybe even cruise some of the back roads just
in case she *was* stranded somewhere . . . but if she got back
to the house and found he and Heather missing, she'd be
worried. And she'd be alone there, not even aware that she
was in danger.

Bill Mullen's big wrecker went by just then, towing a
badly battered import that looked as though it had rolled,
windshield shattered, driver's door twisted half off, clots of
dirt and grass trailing from it. Dev gave his head a shake and

was just going to pull out from the curb when it hit him like a fist in the stomach—Jess's car. That import dragging behind Mullen's wrecker looked like Jess's rental car!

He put the truck in gear and pulled out from the curb and into a sharp U-turn that earned him a shouted obscenity from some kid in a cherry-red pickup. The wrecker was just turning into Mullen's Autobody and Dev careened in behind it, nearly running over one of the mechanics who came wandering out to have a look. He jumped out of the way with a shout and Dev slammed on the brakes and cut the engine, then he was out of the truck and racing across to where the wrecker was lowering the mangled car.

"Where did you find it?" Dev shouldered by a couple of onlookers as Mullen got down from the cab. "Where's the driver?"

Bill Mullen shrugged, shifting a wad of tobacco. "Dunno. Just got a call to come out and pick it up—some kid found it 'bout half an hour ago, out on Smuggler's Cove Road."

"The driver, damn it—where is the driver?"

"Nobody around when I got there—prob'ly someone took her to the hospital already."

"Her?" Dev swallowed, the knot in his belly twisting so tight he could barely breathe. "You're sure it was a woman?"

"Pretty sure. Found this—" Mullen reached into the cab of the wrecker for something, then handed it to Dev: a woman's handbag.

Jess's handbag. He didn't even have to open it to check.

He felt sick and light-headed, struggling to come to terms with what was happening.

"Someone sideswiped her good." Mullen ran his hand almost lovingly along the battered side of the car. "Ran her right off the road—rolled a full three-sixty and landed on her tires."

Dev touched one of the deep dents along the driver's door. Blue paint. Starkey had rented a blue Le Baron.

And Jess? Where in God's name was Jess?

"She could still be out there somewhere," he said between gritted teeth. The blood was pounding in his ears and he reached for the front of Mullen's coveralls and grabbed a fistful of fabric, shoving the man against the side of the wrecker. "She could be hurt—she may have a concussion and just have wandered off. Damn it, didn't you even look for her?"

"Hey, man, take it easy...." Hands came from behind him and grasped Dev's shoulders, easing him back. "The kid saw the whole thing happen—said the driver walked away from it without a scratch. She's okay, man.... Just take it easy now!"

Dev shrugged away from the restraining hands, releasing the front of Mullen's coveralls. The older man stumbled away, looking shaken. "What kid?" Dev demanded, turning toward the man who had held him back. "Was he certain she was all right?"

"Bob Stinson's kid. He was riding his bike over to a friend's place when he saw it happen—"

"The woman, damn it! What happened to the woman who was driving?"

"Just take it easy, okay? The kid said some man had stopped and was helping the driver out of the car. She looked shaken up, but she was walking fine and the kid said she didn't seem to be bleeding or anything. The guy had to smash the window—I guess the frame got twisted when it rolled, and jammed the door—but he got her out okay and into his car. Then he took off, probably to the hospital. If you go up there and check I'm sure that—"

"What kind of a car was he driving?" Dev asked softly. Knowing already, but needing to hear it. Knowing that Jess wasn't in any hospital...

"Blue Le Baron, I think."

The world spun gently and Dev had to close his eyes, fighting for control.

There was a shriek of car tires behind them, the sound of a car door slamming, running footsteps. "Hey, McAllister! Hey, am I glad I found you!"

Numbed, Dev looked around slowly. Jimmy Zacharis, Tulley's one and only deputy, dogtrotted toward him, the lights from his cruiser circling eerily behind him.

"The chief just called in on the radio and said I was to find you quick, McAllister. He went out to your place this morning to tell you something—that guy you was looking for, what was his name...Starkey? Well, he's on the island. And—"

"I know." Dev's voice was just a hoarse whisper.

Jimmy saw the mangled car just then and stopped, blinking at it. Then he looked at Dev. "Anyway, Tulley says you'd better get out to your place real fast. There's some kinda trouble going on out there and—"

But Dev didn't wait to hear the rest.

Heather.

She was in a small corrugated toolshed of some sort. It was pitch-black and the air was thick and humid and reeked of oil. And it was hot. Sickeningly hot. Jess pulled off her pink sweatshirt and wiped the perspiration off her forehead with her sleeve. Odds were it was going to get a lot hotter as the sun pounded down on the metal roof and walls, and she wiped her face with her arm again, trying not to think of how thirsty she was.

Or how lucky. She touched the bump on her forehead gingerly. Except for a mild crack on the head and a sore shoulder where she'd been flung against the safety harness, she'd walked away from the accident without a scratch.

She looked around the shed. If this could be called luck. She'd been too dazed and shaken up to put up more than a token fight when Starkey had smashed the window of the car and dragged her out, and she'd found herself locked securely in here—wherever *here* was—before she'd had time to really comprehend what had happened.

As her eyes adapted to the dark, she looked around her small prison again. Tall metal storage shelves ran the perimeter of the shed, and the entire place was littered with tools and grimy engine parts, oil drums, cans of rust inhibitor and various solvents, boxes of spare parts and what looked like part of an outboard motor.

She closed her eyes, fighting panic, and took a deep breath. Her presence of mind was the only weapon she had, and she couldn't afford to squander it on hysterics. Stay calm, she told herself fiercely. He can't kill you as long as he thinks you know where the money is. Just stay calm...think it through.

All she had to do was play along with him. Just until Dev got there. She just had to hang on until Dev got there....

Dev made the thirty-minute drive back to his place in a little under fifteen. Frankie's old truck was in the yard and, sitting beside it, blue and red lights lazily revolving, doors agape, was Tulley's police cruiser.

Frankie was sitting on the ground with her head in her hands and Tulley was in the cruiser, talking into his radio.

"What the hell's going on?" Dev demanded. "Where's Heather?"

Frankie looked up slowly, her weathered face gray under the tan. There was blood in her hair and along one cheek. "He was waiting for me. Didn't even have time to pull my Winchester out from under the seat of the truck...."

A wave of sickness hit Dev and he put his hand on the roof of the cruiser to steady himself, feeling dizzy and hollow and numb. He closed his eyes and swallowed, hard, trying not to think of those trusting brown eyes gazing up into his. *I won't let anything happen to you...I'll keep you safe...trust me....*

The cruiser rocked as Tulley heaved his bulk out of it. "He had the place staked out," he grunted. "By the signs, he spent the night up in that grove of trees overlooking the house. When you left this morning, he made his move."

"I shouldn't have left her." He'd left the safe house a year ago when he should have known better. Had come back to find...

"I should have known he'd be waiting."

"I came out to warn you that he'd been spotted on the island," Tulley said. "Found Frankie lying on the ground where he'd left her, you and the girl gone. No sign of your lady, either."

"He has her," Dev managed to get out. All he could see was Heather's small face looking up at him that morning. She'd looked at him with the same expression Jess had the day she'd admitted why she'd come to Whiskey Island. *I didn't know where else to go, Dev. You're the only one I trust.*

The only one I trust...

"Thought he might," Tulley said. "There's another problem, too. Your old boss, McDonald, called me this morning to tell me they found the money. Apparently when your lady called to complain about Starkey, she caused quite a stir. The department put their best men on it and found where Elliott hid the cash—all five million." He gave a snort. "He'd stashed it in a safety deposit vault. Not very original, but damned near impossible to find if you don't know what you're looking for."

"Damn!" Dev slammed his fist against the roof of the cruiser. "That money's the only thing that's keeping Jess alive. If Starkey finds out it's gone..." He looked at Tulley, not needing to say the rest.

"We're just going to have to make sure he doesn't find out," Tulley said calmly. "I'm going to need your help, son. This is too big for me 'n' Jimmy to handle alone."

A shudder ran through Dev and he turned his face away, not wanting Tulley to see the horror in his eyes. "No," he whispered thickly. "I wouldn't be any good to you."

"Now you look here, boy," Tulley rumbled. "I'm too old and fat for this kind of action. I've had my weapon out of this holster maybe eight times in thirty-seven years, and it's been fired twice. Jimmy—well, he's a good kid, but he's young and he's green. This is out of his league. Starkey is big-city trouble. It's going to take a big-city cop to bring him in.''

"I'm not a cop anymore, remember?" Dev whispered raggedly. "I don't have what it takes, Tulley. Not anymore. I'm the last person you need out there, believe me." He squeezed his eyes shut, trying to blot out the images: Gary, Laurel, Shelley. They were all there in the darkness of his mind, watching him accusingly. *We depended on you,* they seemed to whisper. *We all counted on you when it mattered and look at us now....*

Some of the color had come back into Frankie's cheeks and she looked at Dev grimly. "I'm real sorry, McAllister. I'm just gettin' old, I guess. He never woulda got me that easy once."

"It wasn't your fault," Dev said hoarsely. "I know Starkey. He's fast and he's mean, and I had no business getting you involved."

"Heather got in the truck and I was just walking around when she screamed. I turned around and he was right there. He said, 'Tell McAllister I've got the kid.' Then he said something about two years in prison . . . and Barney's Marina . . . and that's when he hit me."

Dev swore in a monotonous undertone, bracing both hands on the roof of the cruiser, eyes closed. Jess had trusted him, and he'd let her down. Just as he'd let Gary down, Laurel, Shelley. . . . How much longer was the list going to get? How many more names were going to be added?

"I called the state police," Tulley rumbled, "but they can't get here for three, maybe four hours."

"It'll be over in four hours."

Tell McAllister I've got the kid.

His daughter.

The words ran through Dev like cold water.

And in its wake came the anger. It was hot and strong and it seeped through the chill that paralyzed him. "No," he heard his own voice whisper. "No, damn it, not again. Not this time."

There was only so much a man could take.

The images crowding around him with their whispering voices seemed to ripple and fade and wash away, and suddenly there was nothing there at all but the sound of a bird high in the poplar by the back porch.

He lifted his head slowly, meeting Tulley's eyes, feeling suddenly very calm. "Enough is enough," he said in a dangerously soft voice. "It's gone too far this time. He's got my woman and my child, Tulley. If he wants a piece of me, he's got it."

Tulley's eyes narrowed and he gave a nod. "Then let's make it legal, son," he said quietly. He walked around to the back of the cruiser and opened the trunk, finding what he wanted after a moment and walking back to where Dev was standing. "I like to keep things legal-like. In case there's questions after."

The deputy's badge caught the sunlight and flickered like fine silver as Tulley secured it to the front of Dev's denim work shirt. "Now raise your right hand, son, and I'll swear you in."

Dev only half heard the familiar words, repeating them by rote. He had a sudden sense of disorientation, his mind jumping back nearly twelve years to another place, another ceremony. The words weren't the same but the weight of them on the tongue was, equal almost to the weight of the shield tugging on the fabric of his shirt.

He'd been wearing dress blues back then, everything spit-shined and new. All he could remember, even now, was looking out over the audience and seeing Jess's face gazing back at him, her smile so alive with pride and love it had filled him with its warmth.

She and Gary had been the only ones who had believed in him and his dream. Gary had joined the force two years earlier, too impatient to get his career moving to take the additional degree that Dev had wanted, and he hadn't been able to attend the ceremony because of some undercover assignment. So it had just been Jess there. Just his Jessie....

The whoop of a police siren brought him back to the present with a jolt. He looked around to see Jimmy's cruiser come skidding into the yard in a cloud of dust. He looked down at the deputy's badge. Touched it cautiously. It was solid and real, its weight pulling at his shirt. Not just the weight of the metal, but of everything the badge itself stood for....

How in God's name had he ever thought he could just walk away from it?

Jimmy ran toward them, looking a little pale. "The report you wanted on Starkey came in, Chief. It's even worse than you thought—they figure he's responsible for killing maybe three people, although they can't prove a thing."

Tulley nodded, inclining his head toward Dev. "We got us some help, boy."

Jimmy's gaze fell to the badge glittering on Dev's shirt. He broke into a broad grin. "Sure am glad you're with us on this." He shoved his hand out. "And I don't mind telling you I'm a little scared."

Dev shook the younger man's hand firmly. "Nothing wrong with that," he said quietly.

"I'm not one to criticize a man's choice in weapons," Tulley spoke up from the rear of the cruiser, "but you're packing kinda light, McAllister. Considering what we might be up against. How about something with a bit more firepower?"

Dev walked around to join his new chief. "What have you got?"

Tulley gave him a lazy smile and lifted the lid on the trunk. "Choose your iron, son."

Dev gave a low whistle at the arsenal of semi and fully automatic weapons, some on the borderline of being legal.

He glanced at Tulley, raising an enquiring eyebrow, but Tulley just smiled beatifically and Dev decided this was hardly the time to question his Chief's taste in hardware.

In the end, he picked out a Beretta and a handful of extra clips, securing it in a leather shoulder holster that fit him like a glove. It felt strangely comfortable after all this time and he flexed his shoulders to settle the harness, bemused at how easy it was, after all.

"This kind of stuff is more up your alley than ours," Tulley said. "You tell us what you want, and me and Jimmy will do it."

Dev nodded, eyes narrowed. "First, keep everyone away from Barney's Marina. Starkey will be well armed, and with five million at stake, he won't think twice about killing anyone who gets in his way. Then run a blockade across the mouth of the bay... fishing boats, nets, the dredge, anything that'll float. If he gets through me, I don't want him leaving here with Jess and Heather, is that clear?"

"You just make sure he don't get through you, boy."

"Jimmy, you get Frankie into the hospital, then meet Chief Tulley at the marina. I want both of you there, but well out of firing range, understand? Starkey spent six months as a sniper in the Marines, and he can still dot an i at a thousand yards. Chief, when you're in position, get on the bullhorn and keep him busy—don't get him mad, just let him know you're out there."

"You got it." Tulley had a predatory gleam in his eyes. "Where are you going to be?"

Dev suddenly realized he felt calm, the adrenaline pumping, all the old reflexes and instincts as sharp as they'd ever been. The fear was exactly where it should be—near enough to keep him on his toes, but too well controlled to get in the way—and every sense seemed more alert, more keen. "I'll be there."

Tulley nodded. "We're right behind you, son."

"Then let's rock," Dev said softly. "Let's get it done."

* * *

There were two ways in. Straight down from the front gate, or in from the water.

It would be suicide to try to approach from the gate—the access road dipped sharply down into the marina from the highway and was wide-open, with absolutely no cover. Starkey would have a clear shot at anyone coming down. That meant two things: he'd be expecting Dev to come in from the water, and he'd be hidden somewhere where he could watch both the main gate and the dock.

Dev squatted on his heels on the hillside overlooking the marina and scanned the place slowly with the pair of high-powered binoculars he'd borrowed from Tulley.

It looked deserted. Someone—Starkey probably—had pulled the chain barricade across the entrance and put out the Closed sign, and nothing stirred in the sticky afternoon heat. Finally, satisfied that Starkey hadn't spotted him, he slipped the binoculars inside his shirt and picked up the big pair of bolt cutters and cautiously started making his way down the hillside.

Crouching against the wire mesh security fence that ran the perimeter of the marina, Dev glanced at his watch. Another minute. He wiped the sweat from his face with his arm and looked down at the boats tied up in the marina.

There was a big cabin cruiser that had come in early yesterday. The owner had gassed up at the pump, then had moored in an empty slip, paying by cash. The marina owner had looked at the picture of Starkey that Dev had shown him and had allowed that, yes, it *could* be the same man, although he wasn't ready to swear to it.

But Dev was. The boat was big and flashy, bristling with antennae and fishing gear and tricked out with every navigational gadget and expensive toy there was. And it was fast, outfitted with twin diesel inboards that could outrun anything Tulley could put in the water. It had Starkey written all over it, although how an ex-con fresh out of jail could come up with that kind of money was anyone's guess. Drug money, perhaps. Blackmail. Who knew.

Dev smiled. That was Starkey's problem—he just never knew when to quit. He combined arrogance with a gambler's love of risk, but he didn't have that special intelligence it takes to make the combination work. If he'd been smart, he'd have taken Jess and hightailed it back to the mainland with her before anyone even knew she was gone.

But he hadn't been able to resist the urge to showboat, to go for that extra wattage of risk by deciding to go after Dev, as well. He'd done the same thing two years ago when the investigation team had been closing in on him. Again, if he'd been smart, he'd have stopped all his illegal activities until the investigation was over. But of course he hadn't, arrogant enough to think he couldn't be caught.

That arrogance had cost him his career and two years in prison. Dev's humorless smile widened slightly. It was going to cost him a hell of a lot more this time.

"Hey, you down there! Starkey!"

Dev started slightly as Tulley's voice boomed out over the marina, its already impressive power boosted by the bullhorn. In spite of himself, Dev had to grin. That should get Starkey's attention!

"This is Police Chief Tulley, and I'm telling you to come on out of there before someone gets hurt. Now I'm sure we can talk about this, boy...."

Dev lifted the big bolt cutters and started quickly snipping through the mesh of the security fence. All he had going for him was the element of surprise. He had to get through this fence and down into the marina before Starkey realized the flurry of activity up at the gate was nothing more than a distraction.

It took him a good five minutes to get through the fence, and by the time he folded back the two-foot square patch of mesh and eased himself through the hole he'd made, he was certain Starkey had to be onto what was going on. He paused on the inside of the fence to scan the marina quickly with the binoculars, wondering if Starkey had him in the cross hairs of a rifle scope right now. If he'd even hear the shot that brought him down.

But it never came. And Dev realized, with a tightly exhaled breath of relief, that Tulley's little show up at the gate was working better than they'd anticipated. So well, in fact, that when the shot finally did come it was aimed not at Dev at all, but at the large figure with the bullhorn.

Tulley's voice was cut off in midword, and Dev's stomach tightened as the sound of the gunshot echoed back from the hills across the bay. Damn it, if he'd hit Tulley—

"Now that was right unfriendly, son," came the familiar voice a moment later, edged with a malevolent chuckle. Dev eased another tight breath between his teeth, this one of relief.

"You're making me a little testy, boy," Tulley continued conversationally. "I'm retiring in six weeks, so I'm not real keen on drawing this out. Give me any trouble and I'll just kill you, dump what's left in Whiskey Cove and write you off as a fishing accident, get my drift, son? So why don't you just come on up here and hand over that gun before you hurt someone...?"

Another shot cracked out, but Dev ignored it. As long as he was shooting at his tormentors up at the gate, Starkey wouldn't be shooting at *him*.

He made his way quickly through the maze of storage sheds and outbuildings to the slip where the big cruiser was tied up. The boat rocked gently as he swung himself up and over the rail, and he crouched there for a moment or two, doubting Starkey had brought along help but not willing to take any chances. Not with the stakes as high as they were. He was going to get one chance to free Heather and Jess safely... just one.

When he was certain he was alone, he made his way below deck and found the engine compartment. Then, easing the hatch open, he methodically tore out all the wiring and, as an added safety measure, flung the handful of cabling into the bilge where it vanished under an inch or two of oily water.

He was heading back up on deck when he heard the sound. Pausing with one foot on the companionway, he half turned, frowning, listening hard. Whatever it was, it was coming from one of the bow storage lockers. It sounded like a woman sobbing. Or a child. . . .

The back of Dev's neck prickled. He flicked the Beretta off safety and eased himself through the narrow passageway leading to the bow cabin, pausing in front of the locker doors. Then, bracing himself firmly, he reached out and wrenched the door open.

There was a muffled squeak and something small recoiled into the farthest reaches of the locker, trying to avoid the light. He caught a glimpse of two huge terror-filled eyes and Dev eased his breath out with an oath and lowered the gun, his heart hammering.

"Heather. . . it's me. It's Dev."

There was a static pause, then an explosion of arms and legs as she catapulted herself into his arms with a wail. "Daddy!"

Ten

Dev found himself enveloped in a whirlwind as Heather clamped her arms around his neck and clung to him, trembling and sobbing. He wrapped his arms around her and hugged her back just as tightly, squeezing his eyes closed against a sudden stinging, his throat so thick all he could do for a moment or two was whisper her name.

"Are you all right?" he finally managed to ask her.

Still trembling, she nodded against his shoulder. "H-he hit Frankie and t-told her if I didn't do what he said, he'd hurt Mommy. Is she okay? Is Mommy okay?"

"She's okay," he said tightly.

"And Frankie? Is *she* okay?" Hiccuping, she drew back to look at him, her face streaked with tears and dirt.

Dev smiled reassuringly and eased her to the floor, slipping the revolver back in the holster. "She's got a bump on her head and is spitting mad, but she's fine."

Heather nodded and wiped her cheeks with the back of her hand. "I knew you'd c-come," she said. "I told him you were coming after me and that he'd be sorry, but he just laughed and told me to be quiet." Her eyes snapped. "So I kicked him. That's when he pushed me in that cupboard and locked the door."

It made Dev laugh in spite of the danger they were in, and he gave her another quick hug, thinking of the way Jess's eyes used to snap with anger when she was that age. "Remind me to tell you the story about your mother and the Pulaski brothers one day," he told her with a grin. "But right now we've got to get you out of here. Come on—up on deck. But keep down!"

Heather obediently scurried up the companionway, staying in a low crouch when she reached the deck, seemingly unconcerned by the gun in Dev's hand. "Who were the Pulaski brothers?"

"A couple of bullies twice your mother's size who decided to give her a bad time one day after school when she was...oh, about eight, I guess." Dev eased himself around the end of the cabin and scanned the dock and marina. "Someone told me Jessie was in trouble and I went tearing down to help her. Except by the time I got there, it was pretty much over—she had one of them in tears and the other was hightailing it home with a bloody nose. And from that day on they used to cross the street to avoid her."

Heather giggled, her eyes shining, still scared to death but clearly in control. "You really like Mommy, don't you?"

"Yeah." Dev glanced around at her, managing a rough smile. "She's probably about the most important person in my life, next to you." Although it had taken losing her to make him realize it, Dev reminded himself savagely. What he had to do now was make sure he didn't lose her permanently. "Heather, I'm going to ask you to do something real scary...and I don't have time to argue with you. You're just going to have to trust me, okay?"

She nodded without hesitation, slipping across to stand beside him, and Dev crouched beside her. Sweat was running into his eyes and he dashed it away with his arm, then pointed to where he'd cut through the security fence.

"See that hillside over there? At the bottom, right where that red-and-white rowboat is sitting, there's a hole in the fence. Now we're going to go to the end of the dock, then I want you to light out and run for the fence as hard as you can, keeping well down behind that row of boat trailers so Starkey can't see you. Then I want you to get through that hole and up the hillside without even stopping to look back. There's a trail that goes right to the top, and when you get there, circle around and you'll find Chief Tulley and his deputy. Get inside one of the police cruisers and stay well down. Do you think you can do all that by yourself?"

She gave him a frightened look. "Aren't you coming?"

Dev gritted his teeth. "Your mother's still in here somewhere, Scout—I can't leave until I get her out, too."

"He locked her in that shed." Heather pointed to a small corrugated metal toolshed on the other side of the marina.

Dev gave her a startled look. "Are you sure?"

Heather nodded, her expression intent. "He has a big padlock on it. He unlocked it so Mommy could see I was all right, then he locked it again." She looked at Dev admiringly. "Boy, was she mad. I didn't even know she *knew* those words!"

"Your mother can hold her own," Dev said with a faint smile. Then he looked down at Heather seriously. "Ready?"

She gave a decisive nod. "Ready."

He never should have doubted she could do it, Dev realized a minute or two later as he watched his daughter sprint across to the fence, keeping low the way he'd told her. She had the same steel running through her as her mother, with a healthy dose of McAllister stubbornness to temper it, and he found himself smiling as he watched her slip through the hole in the fence and then take off up the hillside like a jackrabbit.

But it wasn't until she had disappeared into the dense shrubbery and trees at the top that he relaxed, easing his breath out, and dashed the sweat out of his eyes again. One down, one to go. Although getting Heather out this easily had been sheer good luck, he reminded himself. And luck didn't usually strike twice.

The marina was still and quiet. Tulley, obviously watching through binoculars, had kept up a running dialogue to distract Starkey while Heather had been making her getaway, but once the girl had reached safety, he'd fallen silent. Dev hoped the old man's voice had just given out and that it wasn't a sign that one of Starkey's shots had found its mark.

"Starkey!" Dev's voice echoed and reechoed eerily. "It's McAllister. Just the way you wanted it."

It didn't take Starkey long to spot him. The rifle bullet ricocheted off a boat hitch not four inches from Dev's left ear and went singing off into the shadows even as Dev hit the ground and rolled for cover, swearing. He wriggled under the hull of a little cabin cruiser that was still sitting up on the trailer she'd been brought in on, trying to figure out where the shot had come from.

And then, suddenly, he saw him.

Starkey had chosen an almost perfect place to hide. He was in a big open-fronted boat storage shed that had a clear view of most of the marina while the deep shadows in the shed, as well as the handful of stored boats and trailers, provided him with cover.

"I have the woman in here, McAllister—start firing, and you'll hit her, not me."

It was only then that Dev saw Jess. She was crouched in the shadows beside Starkey, gagged and probably bound, and Dev eased his finger off the trigger of the Beretta with an oath. "You wanted me, Starkey," he called calmly. "You got me. Let's do this man-to-man. Let Jess go—there's no need for her to be involved."

There was a bark of humorless laughter from the shed. "Not a chance, McAllister."

"She doesn't know where the money is." Dev wriggled from under the trailer and sprinted across to a metal shed, working himself a little nearer to Starkey. "But I do, Starkey. Gary told me just before he died."

There was a long, thoughtful silence. Then, "You're lying."

"Want to take that chance, Starkey?" Dev goaded gently. "Let Jess go, and we'll talk."

Starkey's reply was profane, and Dev leaned around the corner of the metal shed and fired three shots into the shadows where Starkey was hiding, high enough to miss Jess but close enough to Starkey to rattle him.

"You killed Gary Elliott, didn't you?" Dev called.

"Elliott never had the guts to finish what he started," Starkey called back. "I knew from the beginning that it was a mistake to get him involved, but by then I didn't have a choice. And it was exactly like I knew it would be—things started to heat up and he went running to you, just like he always did."

Dev closed his eyes. "You followed him that night."

"Of course I followed him—he was going to spill his guts and take us all down. I knew he was going to meet you, and I knew you'd be alone. You were always predictable, McAllister. A real Lone Ranger. I knew you wouldn't take backup with you."

Dev gritted his teeth, a cold rage sweeping through him.

"After I got there, I went up onto that warehouse and set my shot and waited for you. I wanted to do him while you were watching, see. And I was going to do you, too, but you moved so quick I lost the shot. But hell..." He laughed coldly. "I knew I'd get you sooner or later. It was what got me through those two years in prison, McAllister—thinking about that five million, and thinking about killing you."

"Then let's do it, Starkey," Dev called out coldly. "You don't need Jess. The money's right where Elliott left it—in a storage locker out by the airport—Johanssen Storage and Rental. It's in my name now—I'll toss you the key. Then you can let Jess go and I'll call the local heat off. It'll just be the two of us, Starkey. One on one. How about it?''

There was another thoughtful pause. ''If you really have the money, how come you haven't taken off with it?''

''Gary left the money for Jess and the girl,'' Dev lied. Come on, Starkey, he urged silently. Take the damned bait!

''Throw the key over.''

Dev took the flat key from his pocket, offering a prayer of thanks that it was still there. He took a quick glance around the corner of the shed, then threw it into the shadows where Starkey was hiding. ''Did you get it?''

''I got it,'' Starkey said after a moment.

''Okay, now let Jess go. It's just me you want....''

He wouldn't go for it, Dev knew—even odds weren't Starkey's style. But that was okay. He was just stalling for time anyway, trying to map out the best way in. There wasn't going to be any second chance—he had to do it fast and clean, and he had to do it right.

And he had to do it soon. That key wasn't going to distract Starkey for long. The longer he took, the more time Starkey had to think things through...and that was just going to make him more dangerous.

Dev closed his eyes for a calming moment, taking a deep breath to steady his hands. Then he eased himself to the corner of the shed and dared to glance around, searching frantically for Jess. She was sitting a little behind Starkey with her back against a boat trailer, knees drawn up, eyes wide and dark in the dim light, and he swore under his breath. There was no way he could fire at Starkey without taking a chance of hitting her. Not at this range. He had to get nearer.

He drew in another deep breath, then lunged around the corner and sprinted toward the open shed, ducking and weaving, two images superimposing themselves in the same heartbeat: Jess flinging herself away from Starkey and hugging the ground, and Starkey coming up out of a crouch with his teeth bared, the weapon in his hand blazing.

Dev dove to his right, hard, landing on his shoulder and rolling to his feet, firing from the hip. His shot went high and wide but it made Starkey duck, and in the next instant, he'd lost him. Starkey was there in one heartbeat and gone the next, diving out of the shed and vanishing behind a row of boat trailers and Dev swore with heartfelt fury as he watched his prey elude him.

He took one step to go after him, then stopped. Starkey was headed for the cabin cruiser—and what he thought was a clean getaway. Except he wasn't going anywhere.

Jess was struggling to sit up, her hands bound tightly behind her, looking a little dazed, and Dev wheeled around and was beside her in the next breath. He pulled the gag from her mouth gently, then started untying her hands.

"Heather," she whispered hoarsely. "He has Heather."

"Heather's fine." Dev drew her unbound hands forward and started chafing her wrists to get the blood circulating again. "I got her out, Jess. She's all right."

"Oh, thank God!" The words caught on a sob. "I knew you would. I knew I just had to hang on until you got here...."

"Are you all right? He didn't hurt you, did he?"

Jess shook her head. "J-just scared me to death." She looked around the shed, shivering violently. "Where is he?"

"Gone." Dev glanced outside where everything was still and quiet. "He's trying to make a run for it."

Jess gave him a frightened look. "He could be circling around to—"

"Not now," Dev said quietly. "Not when he knows I'm ready for him. While he had you and Heather, he had the advantage. But it's just one on one now. Even odds. And that's not Starkey's way."

She just nodded, shivering again. Still rubbing her hands and wrists, Dev looked at her, his gaze locking with hers. And in the next instant she'd flung herself into his arms and he was holding her in a fierce embrace, his throat filled with all the things he wanted to say to her. He tightened his arms around her and buried his face in her hair, feeling her heart race against his.

"Jessie," he murmured. "My God, Jessie, I don't know what I'd do if I lost you."

"Do you really think there's any chance of that?" she asked with a sob of laughter.

"I never meant to hurt you, Jessie," he said in an agonized whisper. "All I ever wanted to do was love you...but I just never knew how, damn it! I just never knew how."

"I know, Dev," she murmured. "I know. But it doesn't matter now."

But it did matter, Dev realized wearily. It did matter....

"Dev! My God, Dev, you're bleeding!" Jess pulled back in horror, holding out her blood-smeared hands.

"Damn!" Dev peered down at his left side, not feeling anything that should account for the blood soaking his shirt. He pulled it away from himself, wincing. "It's just a crease—barely even broke the skin." Jess had gone so pale he looked at her sharply. "Don't give out on me now, sweetheart. It's just a nick—a bandage and a shot of Scotch, and I'll be as good as new."

Jess closed her eyes for a moment, nodding, and wet her lips. "Is it really over? I can't believe Starkey backed down this easily."

"It's not over," Dev said grimly, wiping his bloody fingers on his thigh. "He lit out of here because he wants that money more than he wants me. Besides, he figures that with five million bucks in his pocket, he can *hire* someone to get rid of me."

"Is the money really in that locker?"

Dev smiled recklessly. "Nope. McDonald's people found it in a bank vault yesterday."

"You mean that was all just a bluff?" She stared at him in astonishment. "But where did you get the key?"

"It's for Frankie's storage shed," he admitted with a smile. "She left it with me a couple of days ago so I could pick up an old outboard engine that needs repairs."

Jess managed a rough laugh. "So you sent poor Starkey on a wild-goose chase."

"I wagered that the money meant more to Starkey than hurting you," Dev said softly, touching her cheek with the back of one bloodied hand.

"You okay, son?"

Tulley's voice rumbled around them and Dev eased himself away from Jess, nodding. "He'll be on the boat," he said quietly. He stood up and drew Jess gently to her feet. "I have to get him, Tulley. He killed my best friend and he would have killed Jess and my daughter if he'd had the chance. He's mine, and I want him."

"Dev..." Jess put her hand on his arm. "Dev, please...."

Dev looked at Tulley. "Take Jess out of here. And keep Jimmy back, too. I don't want anybody hurt."

Tulley's eyes narrowed on his, as hard as agate. Then, abruptly he gave his head a sharp nod. Jimmy started to protest, then snapped his mouth shut at a look from Tulley. "I'll give you twenty minutes," Tulley said. "If you don't bring him out by then, I'm coming in myself."

Dev nodded grimly, starting to unfasten the deputy's badge on his shirtfront. Tulley reached out and stopped him. His eyes held Dev's calmly. "Don't do that, son," he said softly. "Take that off, and I can't let you go in there. You do it legal, or you don't do it at all."

Dev hesitated, then simply smiled humorlessly and drew his hand from the badge. "If that's the way you want it."

"That's the way it has to be, son," Tulley rumbled.

"Tulley, for heaven's sake, you can't just let him—" Jess bit the rest off as Tulley turned and walked out of the shed without another word. Jimmy followed, looking perplexed and troubled. "Dev..."

"Jess, I have to do it," Dev told her flatly. "If I don't, I'll never be able to live with myself. He killed Gary."

"Gary killed Gary," Jess said with forced calm. "If you go in there and kill Starkey, you're no better than he is."

Dev managed a dry smile. "I'm an officer of the law, remember? I'm just going in to arrest Starkey."

But her eyes told him she knew otherwise. That this went well beyond something as simple as justice. "Damn it, Devlin," she whispered, trying not to cry, "don't you dare go in there playing hero! Not for Gary's sake, and not for mine. I ... My God, Dev, I can't face losing you now!"

"Hey," Dev said softly, cupping her face in his hands, "you're not going to lose me, Jessie." He kissed the tears from her eyes. "I promise you that, sweetheart. Trust me." He kissed her gently on the mouth, then turned away, pulling the Beretta out of his belt.

"Dev...!"

He glanced around. "I have to, Jess. I'm sorry." And with that, he slipped out into the burning late-afternoon sunshine, and headed toward the water.

It would have been easy enough to let him go. A couple of phone calls is all it would take to set up a stakeout at the Johanssen Storage and Rental. Caught with the stolen money in his hands, and with Jess's testimony to back it up, Starkey would spend the rest of his life behind bars. If he even made it that far. Cops who kill cops have a lot of enemies.

But it wasn't that simple. He owed Gary this much. And maybe, in some strange way, he owed it to himself even more.

The big cabin cruiser was adrift when Dev finally worked his way down to the slip. Starkey had obviously slipped her mooring ropes free when he'd come racing aboard, intending to simply kick the big inboards to life and roar out of the marina before anyone could stop him.

Except the cruiser wasn't going anywhere. Not without a complete rewiring.

Smiling a little maliciously, Dev eyed the gap between the dock and the cruiser, then took a deep breath and jumped.

He made it, but just barely. Swinging himself over the starboard rail, he crouched there for a moment or two, gun drawn, then started making his cautious way to the bridge.

He wasn't surprised to find it empty. When the engines didn't start, the first thing Starkey would do was head down to check them. Slowly, but with an odd calmness that seemed somehow unreal, he made his way below deck and down to where the engine access hatch was located.

Starkey was there. Crouched by the side of the open hatch, he was simply staring at the destruction as though unable to believe what he was seeing. Dev looked at him for a moment, then raised the revolver and stepped forward.

"She's not going anywhere, Starkey," he said very quietly.

Starkey froze. And then, very slowly, still on one knee, he turned to face Dev. His face was slick with sweat and he was breathing fast, and for half an instant all Dev could see was Martin Conroy's face, the same look of trapped terror in his eyes. He thought of Heather, of Jess . . . of Gary. And, not saying a thing, he leveled the revolver at the other man's chest.

"You won't kill me," Starkey said harshly. "I know you, McAllister—you're too good a cop."

"You think so?" Dev smiled coldly. "I'm not a cop anymore, remember? I burned out, Starkey. I took Martin Conroy out in cold blood, just like you killed Gary. I can take you out the same way, call it self-defense . . . you really think Tulley will say otherwise?" He walked around and kicked the hatch closed, watching Starkey flinch.

"You're nothing to Tulley but a minor irritation. If I arrest you, it'll mean paperwork and court appearances from now 'til Christmas. He's retiring in two months—trust me, Starkey, he doesn't want the aggravation."

Starkey swallowed, seemingly mesmerized by the gun pointing at him. "You can't do it, McAllister," he whispered. "I know you."

"Once, maybe," Dev said with another cold smile. He reached up and took the deputy's badge off his shirtfront and tossed it onto the deck in front of Starkey. "You made a big mistake when you got Jess involved, Starkey. You made it personal then. But your biggest mistake was kidnapping my daughter."

Starkey was staring at the badge. He was sweating heavily now, and he swallowed again, wetting his lips as he looked up at Dev stupidly.

Dev smiled companionably. "That's right, Starkey. Heather is my little girl."

Starkey's mouth worked but no words came out. He stared at the gun in Dev's hands in dazed fascination, his face gray under the slick of sweat, and Dev could smell the fear on him.

For a heartbeat of time, Dev didn't know himself what he'd intended to do. He found himself lifting the revolver slightly and sighting down the barrel, seeing Starkey's fear-contorted face . . . and, lying on the deck, the discarded badge. Feeling all the pain and helpless rage well up through him again as he thought of holding Gary on that moonlit dock while his life slipped away.

And then he thought of Jess, and a wide-eyed little girl who had called him Daddy. . . .

And suddenly, he lowered the revolver with a snort of disgusted laughter, giving his head a rueful shake. "Hell, Starkey, you're not even worth it."

There was a shout outside, the whoop of a police siren, and Dev motioned for Starkey to get on his feet. "You're under arrest. And when the courts get through with you this time, you're going to be behind bars until hell freezes over."

He stood on the dock and simply let the sunshine soak into him, feeling it ease muscles he didn't know were tight, aches he didn't know were there. His side, where Starkey's bullet had creased him, was starting to hurt like blazes now, the shock wearing off, but he found himself almost relish-

ing the pain. Feeling alive—really alive—for the first time
in nearly a year.

Jimmy was hustling around being officious, reading his
prisoner his rights and playing around with handcuffs and
confiscating weapons. Tulley just stood back watching, offering a word of advice now and again and scratching his
ample belly with a look of contentment, as though generally
satisfied with the world.

She was waiting for him at the end of the dock, hugging
herself and looking pale and frightened. When he strode
toward her she lifted her head and he could see the glitter of
tears on her cheeks, smiled as she hastily wiped them away
with the back of her hand. Still his Jessie, hating to let him
catch her crying.

"Hi." He grinned down at her, suddenly feeling about
twelve years old again. "You okay?"

"Damn you, Devlin McAllister, you scared me half to
death! Don't you ever, *ever* do anything like that again, do
you understand me?"

It would have been perfect if her voice hadn't broken on
the last word. She bit her lip to stop the spill of tears but it
was too late, and when he reached for her she flung herself
into his arms with a sob.

"No, ma'am," he promised, laughing softly. He tightened his arms around her and buried his face into her sweet-
scented hair, wondering how in God's name he'd ever lasted
those eight long, cold years without her. "How's Heather?"

"She's fine," Jess sobbed. "Better than I am!" She
managed a breath-caught laugh, wiping her eyes on his shirt.
"Y-you'd think I'd be used to being scared to death, putting up with you and Gary for most of my life! If it wasn't
motorcycles, it was fast cars or scuba diving or speed-
boats...."

"Hey," he teased, "I'm a cop, remember? I can do this
sort of thing in my sleep. If you're going to be my wife, you
can't fall apart like this every time I go out on a call."

"Maybe you can do this sort of thing in *your* sleep, but—" She stopped suddenly. Looked up into his eyes. "What did you say?"

Gazing down into those melted-chocolate eyes, feeling her heart beating against his, the warmth of her body tucked in close to him like this, Dev wondered why he'd ever had any doubts. It was so easy, he mused. So easy to just come out and say, "I love you, Jessie."

She looked so thoroughly stunned that Dev had to laugh. "I know it's taken me a long time to get it through my thick head, but letting you get away from me was the biggest mistake I ever made. And I've spent eight years blaming you, blaming Gary—blaming everyone but myself."

He kissed her gently. "When I was in there looking down the barrel of that gun at Starkey, I realized two things, Jess. The first is that I didn't shoot Martin Conroy in cold blood. I came up behind him and got the drop on him, all right, but he spun around and fired at me . . . it *was* self-defense."

He gazed down at her for a moment. "And the second thing was that there is absolutely nothing in the world more important to me than you. Not Starkey, not Gary . . . none of it."

"Oh, Dev . . ." It was just a whisper, filled with wonder.

"And I realized something else, too—that if I lose you this time, I've lost you for good. You're not going to sit around for another eight years waiting for me to make up my mind about whether I love you or not, whether I want some kind of lasting relationship or not. You're going to find some other man and make a life without me, and I'm going to be out in the cold with a part-time daughter, if I'm lucky, and a lot of regrets. And I wouldn't even have Gary to blame this time."

He gave a snort of laughter. "Hell, Jessie, I've loved you since I was twelve years old. I figure the universe gave old Devlin McAllister a second chance—and I'm not going to mess it up this time. I'm going to grab you while the grabbing's good. I want to be your forever man, Jess. I want you to marry me.''

"Of course."

He gave her a slow, lazy smile. "That easy, huh?"

"I've only been waiting about fifteen years, Devlin," she reminded him dryly. "You've *always* been my forever man."

She lifted her lips for his kiss and Dev sank into the sweetness of her with a sigh, trying to ignore the large, khaki-clad figure strolling nonchalantly toward them. "Go away, Tulley," he muttered. "Can't you see I'm busy?"

"Well, as much as I hate intruding on a man at a time like this," Tulley replied amiably, "there's one little matter we gotta get cleared up."

Dev sighed, giving Jess one last lingering kiss before lifting his head to look at the other man. "This had better be good."

Tulley just shrugged, turning something bright in his fingers for a moment. Then he flipped it toward Dev. "You musta dropped this."

The sun glinted off the police shield as it tumbled through the air and Dev caught it easily. "Yeah." He smiled, holding Tulley's deceptively sleepy gaze for a long moment. "I must have."

"I was talking to my wife last night, and she allowed as to how she'd like to take a little vacation this summer. Down to Colorado to visit our son. His wife's having a baby any day now."

"Sounds nice," Dev said mildly. "Colorado's great this time of year. Good fishing, too, I hear."

"Yep. Trouble is, she wants to go down right away. To help out with the new baby, see. Told her I'd sure like to, but Jimmy's too young to be left all on his lonesome. She suggested I find someone to fill in for me for a few weeks...."

Dev turned the shield in his fingers, letting the sun catch it. "Have anyone special in mind?"

"Might have." Tulley gave a rumbling laugh, scratching his belly like a dog in the sun. "Hell, boy, sounds to me like you're going to need a decent job, with a wife and daughter and all.''

Dev gave a long, lazy laugh, cradling Jess against him. "What do you think, Jessie? Figure I can handle the job?''

"I think you were born to the job,'' Jess murmured, standing on her tiptoes to plant a kiss on his cheek. "Chief of Police Devlin McAllister...has a nice ring to it, don't you think?''

"Speaking of rings, Mrs. Jessica McAllister-to-be,'' he murmured, "after I get this hole in my ribs patched up and we get that bump on your head looked at, how would you like to celebrate this auspicious day with a visit to the nearest jeweler?''

Jess gave a peal of laughter. "Once you make up your mind to do something, you don't waste any time, do you?''

"Not this time,'' he growled. "I want you in permanent protective custody, lady. And the sooner the better!''

Epilogue

"Hey, Mrs. McAllister?" George Busby stuck his head in the open door and peered around the corner at Jess. "The Chief in?"

"He's outside, George. Do you want me to call him?"

"Nope...just brought that lumber he ordered first of the week. Where do you want it?"

Jess took the last pan of cookies out of the oven and slid it onto the cooling rack, then walked across to the door. "Just put it out in the shed, George, thanks."

George nodded and held the door open for her as Jess walked out into the sunshine. "Chief adding another room or two, is he? I...uh...heard the good news."

Jess smiled. "Not exactly. He's just building something for Heather. Would you like a cup of coffee?"

"Oh, no, ma'am, thanks." He touched the peak of his cap. "Got three more deliveries. Be seein' you."

Jess watched George drive off in a cloud of dust, then picked up a handful of chocolate chip cookies and walked across the yard and down the hillside to where Dev was working. Teddy was sprawled out under the tree and he bounced to his feet when he saw her, tail wagging.

"Not a chance," she told him dryly as he eyed the cookies in her hand. She walked across to the big tree and looked up into the canopy of green.

Dev had the floor down and was working on one of the walls now, sawing and hammering industriously. He'd made the ladder already, a sturdy, no-nonsense wooden affair secured to the trunk of the big tree, and Jess, balancing the cookies in one hand, made her way up easily.

Dev was measuring a length of planed pine, stripped to the waist and barefooted, his tanned torso gleaming like gold in the speckled sunlight filtering through the leaves. He glanced around as she came up onto the platform and swore with surprise. "Jess!"

"Hi." She grinned at him. "Thought you might be ready for a break."

"For crying out loud, Jessie," he muttered, taking the cookies with one hand and grasping her arm gently with the other, leading her into the center of the platform. "You shouldn't be climbing trees! Not in your condition."

Jess arched an eyebrow and reached out to take one of the cookies from his hand. "Devlin, I'm not in a *condition,* I'm simply pregnant. Barely seven weeks pregnant, to be exact." She gave her flat, denim-covered stomach a pat. "And young Gary may as well get used to climbing trees—when you get this tree house finished, every kid in the neighborhood will be living up here."

"Gary." He nodded, munching thoughtfully. "I like that. I think the original Gary would like it, too."

Jess smiled and reached up to brush crumbs from Dev's mouth. "I know he would," she said softly. "We... umm... got a letter today. From Shauna."

"My baby sister?" Dev looked at her in surprise.

Jess smiled. "Your baby sister's getting married in a couple of months. She wants you to give her away."

"Married?" He sputtered. "She's just a kid, for crying out loud!"

"She's twenty-seven," Jess reminded him dryly.

He gave a grunt. "Who's she marrying? Not that good-for-nothing Mills kid from down the street?"

"That good-for-nothing Mills kid is a doctor now," Jess told him patiently. "Pediatrics, I think."

"A doctor?" Dev shook his head, raking his fingers through his hair. "Do you get the feeling we're getting old, Jessie?"

"Just getting better," she reassured him. "We also got a letter from Tulley. He says the fishing's just fine in Colorado, and that he's thinking of staying another month or two."

"Old bandit," Dev rumbled. "You can write and tell him it's safe for him to come back now that the election's over and it's official." He nodded to where his khaki shirt, with the shiny police chief's shield on the pocket, was hanging on a nearby branch.

Then he chuckled, giving his head a shake. "That fat old man had me sized up five minutes after he met me."

"Sorry you took the job?"

Dev grinned down at her. "What do you think?" He kissed her lightly. "What about you? Any regrets about becoming the wife of the local chief of police?"

"I love a man in uniform," Jess teased, running her hands up his bare chest. "Although," she added with a mischievous, upswept look, "I kind of like this particular one even when he's out of uniform...."

Dev's smile widened and he slipped his arms around her, pulling her close. "Remember that afternoon on your nineteenth birthday?" he murmured, nibbling the side of her throat. His hands were warm and strong as he caressed her back and Jess felt a little shiver of anticipation wind through her.

"Funny, I was thinking that same thing." She lowered her mouth to the hard nub of his nipple and swirled her tongue around it, feeling his breath catch.

She smiled, drawing her fingertips lightly down his belly to the snap on the waistband on his jeans. "Heather won't be home from school for at least two hours," she murmured, drawing the zipper down very slowly. She looked up at him through her lashes and found him gazing down at her, his eyes glowing with that deep hunger she loved. "And no one can see us up here...."

"I think seducing the chief of police is some sort of felony," Dev whispered, starting to tug her shirt out of her jeans. "I should probably arrest you...or something...."

"Or something," Jess murmured, lifting her mouth for his kiss. "I love you, Devlin McAllister. And you *something* so well...."

* * * * *

SILHOUETTE·INTIMATE·MOMENTS

NORA ROBERTS
Night Shadow

People all over the city of Urbana were asking, Who was that masked man?

Assistant district attorney Deborah O'Roarke was the first to learn his secret identity . . . and her life would never be the same.

The stories of the lives and loves of the O'Roarke sisters began in January 1991 with NIGHT SHIFT, Silhouette Intimate Moments #365. And if you want to know more about Deborah and the man behind the mask, look for NIGHT SHADOW, Silhouette Intimate Moments #373.

Available now at your favorite retail outlet, or order your copy by sending your name, address, zip or postal code along with a check or money order for $2.95 (please do not send cash), plus 75¢ postage and handling, payable to Silhouette Reader Service to:

In the U.S.	In Canada
3010 Walden Ave.	P.O. Box 609
P.O. Box 1396	Fort Erie, Ontario
Buffalo, NY 14269-1396	L2A 5X3

Please specify book title(s) with your order.
Canadian residents add applicable federal and provincial taxes.

NITE-1A

Silhouette Books®